REMEMBERING SIMONE

John Swetnam

CHAPTER 1

I was already drunk when I met Simone, even though it was only eleven in the morning. I had arrived at the El Vaquero with MacElwain's letter in my backpack, planning to skim through it and distract myself by watching the rich Guatemalan girls window-shop on the Reforma. The guidebooks describe the Reforma as "the Park Avenue of Guatemala City" because of the expensive shops, but they never mention the El Vaquero, a Guatemalan's version of a Texas hamburger joint. The jukebox, which glowered next to the kitchen, was stocked with marimba music. The *hamburguesas* were served on stale French bread, and the beer was so cold you thought your fingers would freeze to the bottle.

At ten o'clock I thought a single beer would be sufficient preparation for MacElwain's latest intrusion into my life. By the time Simone arrived, the letter had disappeared into a pleasant alcoholic flush. It existed only as an irritating sense that there was some reason my lips felt numb so early in the day.

I was twenty-four in 1970, with two years left on my draft deferment and a National Science Foundation grant to study the ecology of subtropical moths. It all seems romantic in retrospect, leaving a rented adobe room at dusk to drive my jeep into the forests on the slopes of an extinct volcano. My base was a village where women wove the clothes they wore and men scuffed their sandals in the dirt of the roads as they walked to the fields. During the afternoon, I catalogued the collection from the night before, filling out mimeographed forms detailing the location, temperature, humidity, phase of the moon, and surrounding biota for each specimen. I lived in the sensuous thrall of routine, dazed from lack of sleep, engrossed in the details of a project I neither cared about nor understood.

I looked forward to my trips to the capital every two weeks with anticipation out of proportion to the prospect of a fifty-mile drive to a grimy industrial city. If I was lucky, my postal box would contain no letter from MacElwain, and the Palacio de Revistas would have received a new shipment of English language magazines. To others, MacElwain might have seemed to be a modest academic, but I was exposed to his elegant tyrannies, his constant vanity and his unending crusade to assert his significance in the world of entomology.

MacElwain's career was built upon the improbable claim that temperature, not light, was the key to the daily and seasonal cycle of insect populations. It was the rock upon which he founded his existence, the touchstone against which every datum was tested. This single-minded devotion embroiled him in a world of attacks, slights, innuendos, advances, and defeats. His attitude toward every other biologist was set by the fixing that individual took on this pole star. Since the vast majority of entomologists regarded thermal determinism as either oversimplified or idiotic, MacElwain's universe was a hostile one. As his student, I was expected to carry on his great work to its conclusion.

I shared the general view of MacElwain as a desperate and insignificant man who had won his tenured position in the department at Berkeley largely because he was 4-F during World War II and the department was desperate not to lose any faculty member who could breathe. When they returned from the war, the other department members, men of scholarship and achievement, did not conceal their disdain for his abilities. Students attended his seminars only when departmental requirements could be filled in no other way. I was his only advisee, and I was his student simply because I hadn't bothered to fill out a graduate adviser form my second semester and was too apathetic to protest my assignment to him.
The great mystery of the department was his ability to win one grant after another to pursue his research, in Iran in the early fifties and then in Guatemala. As I perambulated through school, shielded from the Vietnam War by my deferment, I came to see MacElwain as the price one paid for being alive and safe. He represented the revenge of a universe on those who would not directly confront the rigors of survival.

Simone, of course, would have found him contemptible, but I had no way of knowing that when I saw her enter the gloom of the El Vaquero and stumble into the stuffed longhorn which lurked there. Everyone did the first time they saw the place because the rectangle of light cast through the doorway fell just short of his front hooves. Vicente, the owner, had purchased the animal from a University of Texas football fan from Austin who had gone broke trying to export avocados to the United States. The enormous spread of its horns and the baleful glare of its glass eyes often sent tourists recoiling into the street and bought an involuntary grunt from even the most stolid novices. Simone simply put out her hand to pat the animal's nose, and let it slide along the spine as she walked on. When she reached the tail, she lifted it and peered underneath to determine whether this bull was completely equipped. I burst into applause.

She curtsied and sat down two tables away.

She was wearing the uniform of the student traveler of the 1960's, though both of us would have stridently denied any suggestion that we were conformist. Her dark brown hair reached to her shoulder blades, her fatigue jacket was frayed at both elbows, and her faded denims were patched at the knees with red bandana cloth. Still, she didn't seem brassy, or druggy, or jaded. There was a vulnerable quality, and I realized that she was much younger than I, perhaps no older than nineteen.

The perception was new and far from unpleasant. When I had entered graduate school three years before, I had suffered from the illusion that I was growing up, but my position at the bottom of the departmental hierarchy made me realize that every student, no matter his age, is treated as a child. Before me sat someone both sexy and immature. It made me feel like a rogue, and I began to plot my approach as if I were a veteran. My brains felt as if they were sloshing around in my skull, so I took another pull on my beer and groped for an opening.

"Why don't you sit over here with me?" she asked.

"Great," I replied and knocked over two chairs on my way to her table. So much for the smooth conversational entrée. "I'm Jim Fletcher."

"Jesus, it's good to meet someone real. I thought I'd only find tourists here."

Vicente came over and she ordered two beers with an accent that put mine to shame, then lit a Marlboro and shot a blast of smoke toward the ceiling as she leaned back in her chair.

"I stopped at the Panamerican Hotel for breakfast," she said, "and the woman at the next table kept asking the waitress if her pineapple had been washed in purified water. So, the waitress brought her a glass of water. The old bitch nearly lost it. She kept pointing at the pineapple and saying '*agua purificada, agua purificada.*' So, the waitress brought her a pineapple soda, you know, an *agua gasiosa*. In the end she left without paying and the manager came over and chewed the waitress out. As if the whole world should wash in purified water. What does she think the pineapple is drinking in the field?"

"Sounds like a real bitch," I agreed, staring unabashedly at the curve her breast made under the pocket of her jacket.

"Tourists," she said, spitting out the word as if she had a hair on the tip of her tongue. "They're all the same. They come to Tecpan in buses to see the market on Saturdays. The minute they step into the street the women start complaining about the smell of the public john and the men start talking about selling condominiums with a view of the mountains. Then they file into Ramon's gift shop and buy those god-awful shirts with the quetzal birds embroidered on them. Ramon is a Ladino from the capital who treats the Tecpanecos like shit, but because he wears an Indian man's shirt from Nahuala and won't bargain, they think they're dealing with the real thing. They pay four times the market price for blankets from Momostenango. I heard Ramon telling one woman that he wove them himself. They load back on the bus and head for a first-class hotel in Antigua telling one another how lucky they are to be born American."

She absolutely swept me away. Everything about her was exciting and new. She swigged the beer straight from the bottle with deep masculine gulps, her throat pulsing with energy. She sprawled back on her chair with an air of total command. I felt if I hurled myself across the table, took her in my arms, and consummated a sexual act of total spontaneity, she would be as unsurprised as she was by the stuffed longhorn. Even her tendency to long, ornate speeches, which in retrospect I recognize as the product of adolescent insecurity, appeared an affectation of the most amusing originality.

"Yeah," I muttered. The beers made my tongue thick, and I found myself blinking even through the dim atmosphere of the El Vaquero. If only I could match her discourse with my own, express the easy and general contempt for everything the world had to offer. Maybe if I had something to eat, I could clear the buzzing in my ears. Had I taken a sponge bath this morning? Did my armpits smell? My breath must be pretty awful. What if I puked on the tabletop?

"Let's get a couple of hamburgers," I said. "They come with this weird salad that has pickled pullets' eggs sliced on top. I could buy if you're short of money." One of the advantages of living in Palin was there was nothing worth buying that cost more than fifty centavos.

"Thanks," she said. "I'm always short of money. They don't give papal volunteers a stipend, so I have to live off what I can scrounge from Father Mike."

Papal volunteer?" Trouble. Was she some kind of nun? My eyes slid guiltily up from her breasts, but I could hardly look her in the eye. As a result, my focus stranded on her chin.

"You must be a Protestant," she exclaimed.

"Is that bad?" I asked, hastening to add, "I'm not anything really. I haven't been to church in years."

"That's OK. I've dated lots of Protestants. It used to drive the nuns at school crazy. To hear them talk, you'd think all Protestant boys are sex-crazed assassins. Of course, to listen to the nuns, you'd think that all men are sex-crazed assassins."

"I'm one," I said. "Aren't you?"

"I've never assassinated anyone," she said, pausing to give her statement the air of an admission of failure, "and I never sleep with a man until the second date. We Catholic girls have our standards. Sister Peter Marie, the nun who taught health and hygiene, was most clear on that point."

"Can I count this as the first date?" I asked. Just then the waiter came back with the hamburgers, and the conversation slowed as we pitched into the food. She ate the way she drank, with a kind of fierce affection. I wasn't sure what a papal volunteer might be, but as long as vows of chastity weren't involved, I was game to play.

When I look at Simone's picture now, it's a shock to realize how undistinguished her features are. In the cracked black and white snapshot, she looks like, well, a girl just out of high school – shabbily dressed, with hair that is a little thin and stringy and a nose that is a bit too long. Like sailors of an earlier age made desperate by deprivation, did I mistake a manatee for a mermaid? Did I project into that pleasant but hardly exceptional body the lusts that cannot be adequately satisfied by the Playmate of the Month? Logic would indicate that this could be true, but no picture could catch Simone in motion or record the bright self-assurance with which she brought off the most mundane activities. Simone made everything she did uniquely her own.

"You call this a date?" she said, picking up the conversation where it had died, "Casual conversation in a sleazy bar?"

"How about casual conversation in the sleazy movie theater across from the immigration office? *The Moscow Letter* is playing, starring Richard Boone. They say it's the best thing he's done since *Have Gun, Will Travel*."

"That would count if you paid for my ticket," she said, "but I don't have time today. The Flor de Mi Tierra bus leaves in an hour. Are you going west on the Panamerican Highway? Do you have wheels? Maybe you could give me a lift."

"Sure, how far is Tecpan anyway?"

"A couple of hours."

"Then there's time for another beer."

"Great. We can pick up Father Mike at the Terminal Market. You'll really like Father Mike. Everybody does."

My hopes of consummation in the shade of a roadside tree faded. "Father Mike. Just the man I wanted to come along."

"You *are* a Protestant." She said. "Don't worry. He won't start running a bingo game in the back seat."

"There are better uses for back seats."

"Oh," she said, and then she blushed. I needed that blush, needed to catch her off guard. It made me her equal in a game, and the fact that it came after such an innocuous allusion made it all the more meaningful. I had been feeling out of my league as we bantered, and it wasn't just the beer that made me feel slow. Her blush whispered to me of an underlying innocence, an adolescent world of longings for unattainable movie stars and football captains. With that brief, involuntary cardiovascular response, she had restored me to the place of power and control, promising the outcome of our encounter would not take place on alien or threatening ground.

I leaned forward to kiss her. Through my drunken glaze, I had the feeling that this was the moment, but she clutched my arm.

"My God," she whispered, "It's her!"

"Who?"

"The Purified Water Lady."

The figure that appeared in the brilliant square of tropical sunshine at the Vaquero's doorway was ordinary enough. I expected a dowdy matron with wisps of graying hair framing a petulant face. Instead, I saw an attractive woman in her late forties, dressed in expensive sportswear, the kind of clothes my mother might wear to a state park.

"Let's see what happens when she bumps into the steer," I whispered.

"She's coming in too slowly," said Simone.

"There's always hope that he might charge and gore her to death," I said, but Simone was right. The Purified Water Lady's entrance was so tentative that she was able to see the longhorn before her trailing foot left the sidewalk. She sidled around it on our side and advanced in our direction.

"Bandits at seven o'clock," whispered Simone. "Dive! Dive!" She slid back her chair behind her and crawled under the table. The chair teetered, then crashed. I was left with a grand view of her blue jeanned bottom sticking out from under the Masonite tabletop.

"Pap, pap, pap, pap, pap!" Simone squeezed almost inaudible rounds into the advancing form of the Purified Water Lady. "The bullets are bouncing off like raindrops! She must have a new kind of armor plating!"

The Purified Water Lady drifted to a halt in front of our table and stuttered as if she was deciding to address us in English or Spanish. Either she didn't notice Simone or was trying to ignore her.

"Do you know…" she began, speaking slowly and distinctly as if to a small child of limited intelligence. "Do you know whether the food here has been washed in purified water? I asked the man at the travel agency to recommend a restaurant and he said the

El Vaquero was the best American cooking outside the Camino Real hotel." She looked at the dingy interior and wrinkled her nose. "You never can tell, can you?"

"Tell her the waiters have dysentery and never wash their hands," floated up from under the table.

"This isn't a bad place," I said. "As long as you don't eat the pullet eggs that come with the salad, you'll be OK. They use export beef and cook it so hard there can't be any problem with the hamburger."

"Why are you doing this to me?" Simone's voice managed a sotto voce wail. "If you love me, you'll kill her."

The Purified Water Lady looked down at Simone. "Have you found your contact lens yet?"

Simone let out a low growl, like a predator trapped by vengeful farmers.

"I know it's upsetting to lose a contact," the Purified Water Lady continued, sinking onto one of the hard wooden chairs. "One time, my daughter, Rebecca, lost a contact lens at school and hunted for 45 minutes before she found it. She was close to tears when she told me about it, but I reassured her. 'People will understand,' I said, 'they already know that you wear contact lenses, so even if you showed up for class with your old glasses on, they'd pay no attention.'"

"Has Rebecca ever considered rhinoplasty?" asked Simone, as she emerged.

"What?"

"I understand that once you've corrected the eyesight, overbite, and bosom, that's the next step."

"Rebecca has perfect features," answered the Purified Water Lady, apparently impervious to sarcasm.

She produced a wallet from the depths of her purse and flipped it open to reveal a picture encased in plastic.

As the Purified Water Lady had asserted, Rebecca had perfect features, arranged on a face of someone thirty pounds overweight. The glare of the flash had washed any color from her cheeks, and her frizzy, permed curls spread her face across the photo. She was standing against uniform background, like a felon in the lineup. The dartboard visible on the wall behind her furthered the impression that we were looking at someone who served as a target.

"Rebecca's father took that picture the night she graduated from high school."

"Is he a professional photographer?" asked Simone.

"No. My husband was in the dry-cleaning business. We owned three stores in Canton, Ohio. Why do you ask?"

"I thought he might specialize in passport photos or something."

I was ready to kick Simone, and I think that even she felt a momentary pang of remorse for the cheapness of the shot. It didn't seem fair to watch her bullyrag this poor woman. They were as mismatched as a German shepherd and a Chihuahua. Watching Simone in action, I feared that I, too, would make some fatal blunder. So far, she acted as if everything I said was droll and delightful, but who knew when she might consign me to the garbage heap for the most casual comment?

"That's real knotty pine," said the Purified Water Lady. "I had it stained with walnut stain to give the game room a more restful feeling."

"Like a cave?" asked Simone.

"That's what Robert used to say," chortled the Purified Water Lady, twinkling with good humor. "What I saw as cozy and warm, he said was dark and confining. What he wanted was 'light and airy,' which I found cold and drafty. We had wonderful arguments about it all the time. Robert hated the things I would bring back when we traveled. 'They look great in some foreign country,' he'd say, 'but when you get them home, they don't fit in. The colors are wrong or the stuff's cheaply made.'"

"Guatemalan crafts are beautiful," I said.

"You're right," said the Purified Water Lady, "but Robert was right too. They just don't look the same when you get them home."

"I want to hear about the wonderful arguments." Simone cut me off. "Did Robert throw things at you? Did he stoop to vile language when he saw the knotty pine had been stained against his will?"

I was appalled, embarrassed, entranced. Part of me longed to join in her raucous derision, to unfairly and unambiguously send the Purified Water Lady to the street in the complete knowledge of my unalloyed disdain. But I was restrained by a vague feeling that it isn't right to hurt people's feelings.

I grew up in a family where people seldom raised their voices. "That's the way people act in the slums," my mother would say. Our arguments took the form of tense, polite confrontations where hedged statements carried the emotional power of physical assaults. Becoming an ally to Simone's flamboyant arrogance would be wandering from a clipped lawn into an untamed tropical garden.

"Rebecca's on duty in the Philippines," said the Purified Water Lady, who either hadn't followed what Simone said or simply decided to ignore her. "She's in the Waves at Subic Bay. Her father and I were so proud she decided to join. We flew to San Diego when she finished training."

"A long way from Canton, Ohio," I said, the inanity of my phrase jangling in my ears.

"Oh, it's a long way to San Diego. It's a long way to roam," sang Simone, under her breath, but she did seem to be settling down.

"Home of the Wright brothers," I added.

"Actually, the Wright brothers lived in Dayton," said the Purified Water Lady. "Canton has the Professional Football Hall of Fame."

"That's got to be good for the town," I said.

"Robert loved to go there. He must have gone a dozen times before he died."

"Oh, I'm sorry," I said, though I already had the sense already that Robert was dead.

"Heart attack," she said. "At least he lived to see Rebecca safely grown." As she spoke, she made a gentle, deprecating shrug of her shoulders, fending off my sympathy before I had the chance to express it.

"Let's have another beer," said Simone, but when Esteban arrived to take our order, Purified Water Lady announced that she would be leaving us.

"I'll eat at the hotel," she said, dipping her head like a bird taking a dust bath. "I'd like to stay and eat with you here, but I'll have to chance the Guatemalan food. The bus for Chichicastenango leaves at two-thirty."

"We understand," I said, and Simone had to swallow another gust of laughter. "Maybe we'll see you again."

"Oh, I'm sure we will," she said. "When you travel in a foreign country you meet all kinds of people from the United States again and again. I guess it's because there are so few Americans here."

As we watched her slide past the steer and back onto the Reforma, Simone jostled my shoulder in a conspiratorial fashion. "You're sweet!" she announced with delight. "I never would have guessed. The Football Hall of Fame!"

"It's better than watching you bait a defenseless widow," I snapped.

"Far from defenseless," said Simone. "She's a tourist, isn't she?"

That was all she said, and I wasn't going to press her. I was satisfied with being sweet, though I wasn't sure of what she meant. We drank a couple more beers and began to talk about the astronauts that were, at that moment, halfway back from the moon in a damaged space craft. We were sure they would run out of air and wondered if NASA had packed a suicide pill.

"They think of everything," said Simone. "Those engineers have to have prepared for this."

"Probably," I agreed, though it hardly seemed likely. Simone seemed so near, so pulsing with life that I was afraid to disagree and reveal a fundamentally flawed quality under the sweet, non-tourist persona she had created for me. I didn't know yet that once Simone classified you as sweet, or a tourist, or interesting, that was what you were, no matter how mundane your behavior might be afterward.

That afternoon my life became terribly simple. I didn't care about my research, or the letter from MacElwain, or the war in Vietnam, or the astronauts in their chill capsule. I just wanted Simone, wanted her with a wolfish intensity born of lonely nights in a peasant village. I wanted her, and I thought I could get her.

Now I am the one who floats far the from El Tejano, separated by over four decades, 23 million minutes, from the Masonite tabletop and the sight of her healthy throat swilling the cold Gallo beer. It is hard not to give into nostalgia, to identify the alcoholic haze of that afternoon as misty idealism. It's easy to forgive our intolerance, our self-absorbed delight in the lazy disdain with which we viewed those around us. And it's easy to forget, too, that as we staggered back into the bright light of early afternoon, I was pursuing nothing more elegant than a chance sexual encounter with a total stranger.

CHAPTER 2

After we lurched up to the Terminal Market, Father Mike announced in pleasant but incontrovertible tones that he would be driving the first stint on the way to Tecpan. He was probably no more than ten years older than I, but he seemed of another generation. He wore blue jeans, a plaid flannel shirt, and the kind of oxfords mothers buy until their children are old enough to mount an effective resistance. His hair, which was thinning prematurely, was combed straight across his head. The skin of his cheeks stretched tight across his facial bones, giving him the look of a heroic pioneer in a WPA mural. When he smiled at me as he slid behind the wheel of my pick-up, I saw that his teeth, while white and healthy, were crowded out of line.

Father Mike began what was clearly an often-repeated line of chatter as he ground the gears and swung into traffic.

"Everyone knows nuns are terrible drivers, and in the days when they wore habits, there was no problem. People gave them a lot of room. Now they're not so easy to spot and the accident rate is soaring. I understand the Maryknolls have lost three sisters in New York State alone. Priests have never had that advantage, so we're more used to fending for ourselves."

My International Harvester Scout swerved back toward the curb so abruptly I thought we were going to kill several men selling chiclets and cigarettes on the sidewalk. Ahead of us, a pushcart wheezed uphill at a pace slower than a crawl. Father Mike hit the accelerator, passed a diesel truck on the right, then made it back to the center lane, barely missing the peddler while the diesel's worn brakes shrieked behind us.

"I thought I was going to see that guy spread across the windshield," I said, hoping Father Mike would pick up my distress.

"Driving in the city is horrible," he agreed in a cheerful tone as he swung into the extreme left lane to overtake a bus laboring up the slope. "It's a miracle anyone in Guatemala City survives, let alone that the population is growing by ten percent a year."

"I'm not eager to help with the population problem by leaving early," I said as Father Mike downshifted and headed for the curb again.

"If we don't get around this bus, we'll be breathing his exhaust all the way up the mountain."

"Mike believes God protects the devout on the highways of life as well as in the hereafter," Simone announced. "I tell him he ought to get an altar for the Land Rover in Tecpan like the ones in the Guatemalan buses, with the Virgin and Saint Christopher and a million dangling beads." She turned her head and stared at the storefronts flickering by. "Sometimes it helps if you close your eyes."

"For Christ's sake," I exploded. "You could kill somebody." Then after a pause I added, "Sorry for the language."

"I've heard most of the words before," he replied, but he did seem to slow his pace.

"You should hear Mike try to swear," Simone giggled. "He always pauses and has to force the words out. He sounds like a nine-year-old who isn't exactly sure what the body parts do."

"Most nine-year olds I've met could swear like troopers," I said.

"Not in the presence of Sister Angelica," said Father Mike, "at least if they hoped to survive a parochial school education."

They talked like members of a fraternal organization, delighting in the offices, uniforms, jargon, and rituals that separated them from their fellows. Ecclesiastical terms peppered their conversation. "When I tasted Maria's tamales, I thought I would have to administer extreme unction to everyone at the table would meet a response like "you have to give Maria credit; her cooking is the early equivalent of transubstantiation. The most mundane foods come out as having no earthly nature whatsoever." Their language was religious, but good-natured, as if they accepted the absurdity of the institution at the center of their lives.

As Avenida Roosevelt broke free of the outskirts of the city, the traffic slowed to walking pace. Cars in the right and left lanes pinched toward the center, where hard-eyed drivers defended their position in line by packing close to the bumpers in front of them. Except for the sounds of idling engines, the traffic quieted. Radios were turned down, and the aggressive chorus of car horns, which had blared and echoed in the narrow confines of city streets, died away.

"Shucks," said Father Mike. "They're checking identification cards at the guard post. We're going to lose half an hour at least."

"Do they do this often?" I asked. "They always just waved me through on the way to Palin."

"That's because there aren't many Indian towns south of the city," he said. "It seems as if they're always checking for guerillas on the way to the highlands. I hope I remembered to pack my international driver's license. My New Jersey license expired three months ago."

The Scout jerked forward as he popped the clutch to keep a Toyota from edging in front of us.

"Maybe I could switch seats," I offered. "I know my California license is current."

"They never look at the dates," said Father Mike. "Don't worry. I'm sure the international license is in my briefcase somewhere."

By now the cars had formed into a single, irregular line that snaked over the top of a small rise. Once we reached the crest, we could see the road continue down into a steep gully, then begin a winding ascent up the far side, the start of a climb that would take it to the top of the ridge three thousand feet above us.

Even though the dry season was only two months old, the banks that sloped down on either side of the narrow valley were sandy and barren. Dust raised by passing traffic coated the saplings struggling to establish themselves between the rocks. The narrow walls of the barranca seemed to intensify the hush in the line of traffic. Music from car radios died away. The outline of people's heads, seen through rear windows, dipped out of sight and reappeared as drivers dug into their glove compartments for documentation. Like an unruly student sent to the principal's office, the traffic seemed at pains to make a good impression in a situation in which it was already assumed to be guilty.

An unfinished board shack with "PN" (Policia Nacional) painted over the door in crooked, blue letters stood at the edge of the streambed where the highway narrowed to cross a two-lane bridge. Two policemen, holding machine guns, slouched at either side of the road, eyeing the traffic with bored, inscrutable glances. The uniforms were clean and the black leather boots well-polished, but every other aspect of their demeanor was at variance with police efficiency. Their shirts were half pulled out in front, their pants bagged at the knees, and their posture was slovenly and unkempt. The one on the left fingered his weapon with casual contempt.

"I hope the safety is on," muttered Father Mike, echoing my thoughts. He ground the gears and we crept forward. Only a battered Ford pick-up and a Toyota remained before our turn came. "Better get your papers out before we reach this guy," he continued. "I don't want him thinking you're pulling a revolver."

I looked at Father Mike with a new respect. His manner had been so genial I was inclined to dismiss him. Now he was displaying a calm rationality that seemed at odds with religious belief. Simone handed her tourist card across to me, and I put the car papers and my passport with them in the vague hope the seal of the United States on the front would command some sort of deference.

"Uh oh," said Father Mike. "There's some sort of problem up there."

The policemen had snapped to the alert, pointing their machine guns at the Toyota. A third man, also in uniform but one who had a jacket, was standing impassively by the driver's side door, tapping papers in his right hand against his left sleeve. The driver gestured rapidly as he pleaded his case. I could see the officer's head turn to the driver, then focus again on the papers in his hand.

"Could I have left my international driver's license on the bureau?" muttered Father Mike as he pawed through his briefcase. "I'm almost sure I put it back in."

"Maybe we could switch drivers," I said again. "He doesn't seem to be looking our way."

The officer continued to tap the papers with a steady, implacable rhythm. The men with the machine guns were dark-skinned Indians with straight black hair; the officer was fair, with short wavy hair. His hat was pushed back on his head and his face would have looked handsome if it weren't for the tension around the eyes.

"I'll just give him my New Jersey license," said Father Mike. "They never look at the date."

The officer called over his shoulder toward the shack. Five more policemen tumbled out of the hut and ran toward the car. They reached to unsnap the holsters on their belts, so they came at a warped and awkward lope, as if some invisible part of them were missing. One opened the passenger door and leaned across the front seat, jabbing at the driver with an awkward shove.

"What's going to happen?" asked Simone, in a hushed voice.

"If those guys open up with the machine guns," said Father Mike, "Nobody is going to be safe. Maybe you'd better get down."

I felt my shoulders inching upward and back as I suppressed the urge to slide below the level of the dash. This was a time to look like everyone else on the road, and I hoped Father Mike was right about not looking at the date on his driver's license.

One of the policemen snatched the door of the stopped car open and dragged the man from the car so hard he sprawled flat on his stomach onto the roadway. The police gathered around him in a tightening circle, but as he pushed himself to his hands and knees, I could see his face.
He looked young, maybe seventeen, and he gasped in terror. I thought he might begin to cry. One of the policemen kicked him, and he collapsed to the pavement again.

The officer looked down at him with disgust, and walked toward our truck, bringing one of the men with the machine guns with them. Behind him, the remaining police were hauling the driver to his feet and hustling him into the hut. The officer made an indistinct gesture with his hand.

"What does he want?" asked Father Mike.

"I guess he wants us to pull on through," I said.

The Scout lurched forward as Father Mike popped the clutch, and the man with the machine gun raised his weapon, pointing it straight at the windshield of the truck. The Scout halted, and then jumped forward again, grazing the officer's leg. The officer jumped back, and then rapped on the door with annoyance.

"*Las cedulas*," he snapped, asking for our identity cards.

"Here they are, sir," said Father Mike. The machine gun was still pointing directly in our faces. I sat as still as I could. Simone was clutching my sleeve. I felt that any movement, perhaps even breathing too hard, might tempt the police to open fire.

The officer flipped through the passports with disdain, but to my relief didn't even pause to look at the driver's license. The man with the machine gun turned to look over his shoulder, making the muzzle swing in a lazy arc across the windshield. It was so casual and random that one might be accidentally wiped off the planet for no reason whatsoever.

Something was going on in the hut. Two of the policemen who had followed the captive over were jammed together at the small window while another pair crowded the doorway. Like spectators at a prizefight, they jostled each other and commented on the scene they were viewing. Occasionally, all four would flinch at the same time, responding to some unseen violence within.

"They must be working that guy over pretty well," I muttered to Father Mike.

Simone turned and buried her face in my shoulder, but she wasn't crying, just turning instinctively from the event. The machine gun continued to waver back and forth as the guard craned his neck in hopes of seeing what was going on behind him. I wondered whether to say anything, but I was afraid any protest would only make me look more suspicious.

Laughter broke out from the crowd around the hut, a spontaneous shout of amusement and surprise. The soldier twisted further around, held beside our truck by the invisible bonds of discipline, but clearly wanting to join his fellows in watching the fun. I'll never know what happened. A blow struck with exceptional force? The *coup de grace*? Possibly even some spontaneous and heroic bit of defiance that turned the tables, if only for a second, on the unseen inquisitor.

The officer standing by Father Mike looked up across the hood of the truck. Then he handed back the papers in his hands.

"OK," he said in English, pronouncing the last letter as if it rhymed with "sky". He waved us on. Father Mike made his smoothest pull out so far, and we rolled down onto the little bridge over the dry streambed. Mike passed the papers back so his free hand could shift the gears. Simone looked up, though she still fastened an intense grip on my right arm.

"Well, at least we won't have to worry about being stuck behind any slow diesel trucks," said Father Mike, and we all laughed hysterically.

Looking back, I wish I could say we spent the long winding climb up the mountainside depressed and upset by what we'd seen, overwhelmed by the plight of the poor bastard behind us. What I, at least, felt was a blissful sense that we had passed through great danger and emerged unharmed. Simone sagged against my shoulder. I teased her about the marks her grip must have left on my biceps. Even at the top of the mountain twenty minutes later, I could feel where her fingers had dug into the muscle.

Just before we came to the crest, a scenic overlook opened on the left and I told Father Mike to pull over so we could change drivers, because his shifting made me think I would have no clutch plate left. He squeezed the Scout onto the asphalt apron and I took advantage of the moment to walk to the bushes at the side of the road and relieve myself.

"You should just stand beside the car and pee in the road the way the Guatemalans do!" Simone called to me. "I could squat on the other side like the Indian women."

"I'm not sure you can do that in Levis," I said. "Your butt would be waving in the breeze."

"That wouldn't give you any problem."

When I emerged from the bushes, she was standing on one of a line of boulders set up and whitewashed to serves as a guardrail for the overlook. With her feet side by side on the rock, she looked like a little girl traversing stepping-stones in the middle of a brook. Near the top of the mountain, the wind was fresh and cool from the Pacific Ocean to the south, blowing her hair back from her face. She pulled her elbows to her sides against the chill. Below her the ugly smear of the city stretched across the broad valley floor like a spreading fungus, the buildings blending together in the haze of the city's pollution.

"Give me a cigarette," she said. "I hate people who smoke in cars."

It took half a dozen matches before we could get one of my Belmonts to light. We were huddled against the wind, our heads close together. With her face near mine, I could smell the scent of her perfume combined with a rich undercurrent of sweat and body so personal I would have kissed her right then if Father Mike hadn't come over to us.

"I guess I know how the priest and the Levite felt when they passed the man beaten by robbers," he said. "Before the Good Samaritan came along," he added, noting my sense of bafflement.

"What could you do?" I asked, "Take on the whole Guatemalan army?"

"I know," he said. "But I just have the sense we didn't do as much as we could."

Simone patted him on the cheek. "You're sweet," she said.

Now we were both sweet.

"We'd better get going," I said, reaching for the keys. I was sober enough to drive. Simone sat between us, and as I wheeled out onto the Panamerican Highway, she leaned against my shoulder.

"I still think something should be done," said Father Mike. "I'll write to the American embassy."

"What will you tell them?" I asked as we chugged up the last steep slope to the crest of the mountain. "What did you see? One policeman kicks someone he's arrested. Several cops look through a window to see what happened to him after he's taken into custody? They'll just laugh at you."

"If you tell the people at the embassy what happened," said Simone, leaning comfortably against my shoulder, "they'll just feel bad they weren't there to watch. Just like they all wish they were in Saigon, earning brownie points for their careers in the foreign service."

"Still, we can't just do nothing," said Father Mike.

There was hardly an answer to that, so we didn't say anything, but looked toward the crest of the mountain. Once we were over the wooded rise, the city, the police, and the terror would disappear from view, and we could go on to the highlands as if nothing mattered.

That's the way it is when you are young. Each morning creates a whole new universe, and what happened yesterday seems as long ago as the Magna Carta or the fall of Rome. Meeting Simone offered a world of infinite possibility. Tecpan (wherever that was), lay ahead, as did the distinct possibility of a bed on which Simone and I could lie down together. There was no mistaking the comfort she found in contact with my body. So, my heart filled with hope born in the dark confines of a city bar, I drove over the ridge and on into the highlands.

CHAPTER 3

When I had come to Guatemala six months before, I rented the first place I saw – two empty, windowless adobe rooms in a town where the slopes of the volcano met the coastal plane. The front room had a door opening on the street. The back room had a screen door to a cobblestone patio equipped with a cold-water spigot. Still further back was a primitive outhouse. I furnished the back room with a mattress thrown in one corner and the trunk I'd shipped from the United States. I bought a plain wooden table and a straight-backed chair from an Indian vendor in the market and set it by the door to the street. An enormous pile of field paraphernalia, collection bottles, reference guides, uncompleted forms, maps, and examining glasses filled another corner, so I had to trace a narrow path to reach the back room.

My kerosene lantern and cassette tape recorder completed the furnishings. The lantern was always with me, for if I opened the front door to let light in from the street, a knot of children would gather outside to giggle at every move as I worked. The tape recorder ran almost constantly, grinding through the store of tapes I'd brought with me from Berkeley – Beatles, Stones, Buffalo Springfield, and Ravi Shankar. When I slept, I threw myself on my mattress, like a dog curling in its favorite place on a rug.

My meals were cooked by the widow of a schoolteacher who lived a block from the main square. She served me fried eggs, black beans, and tortillas morning and night, and I wolfed them down and wandered off, often without saying a word. Once a week I carried her my dirty laundry at breakfast and she returned it at dinner, two days later, washed and folded.

I'm writing this so you can understand the shock and delight which I experienced as the highlands opened before me. I was like a monk emerging from a winter-long vigil in his cell, blinking in the bright light of springtime. The land bordering the road as it meandered down a gentle slope to the plateau seemed nothing short of paradise.

The way ambled through a rolling country, broken into thousands of tiny fields, some no larger than a suburban front yard, planted in corn, beans, and vegetables. The fields were irregular in shape, and since each had been planted on a different day, given differing amounts of fertilizer, and grew different crops, each had a shade and texture contrasting to the ones around it. Some of the cornfields were sprouting pale green shoots in anticipation of the rainy season to come. In others, last year's stalks were parched, like the effigies of soldiers surrounding the tomb of a Chinese emperor – veterans in death of campaigns to be fought over and over again. Plots near sources of water bloomed with flowers to be sold for the churches in the city – asters, gladioluses, and carnations. On fallow patches, oxen were staked out or a handful of sheep grazed watched by boys no more than six or eight years old.

I had driven through the Midwest and seen fields, caged by barbed wire fences, ploughed and planted in rows as straight as a Lutheran's conscience. As I did my research in the forests, I passed corn fields carved into the side of a mountain wherever a stream or gully deposited a patch of silt. The fields around me as I drove toward Tecpan had neither the desperate, temporary quality of those where men fought the jungle for a year's sustenance, nor the compulsive order of my native land. Here agriculture seemed spontaneous. It was the pine forests on the low ridges in the distance that intruded into a world where man and nature stood as one.

As we rolled along, Simone's spirits lifted with my own, and she chattered about the mission at Tecpan. Perhaps she sensed that to talk about the countryside would make her as superfluous as a tour guide at Niagara Falls, prattling about how many gallons a year flow over the lip and how many households the electrical plant can serve. Instead she talked about what we could not see, and so she prepared me for the mission, a world only slightly less circumscribed than my solitary life at Palin. I only half listened to her, watching for stray livestock which might have wandered onto the road and interjecting a bland question at odd intervals to reassure her that I was attending. Father Mike retreated from the conversation and into the train of thought that was going to have immense consequences in the weeks to come.

The mission consisted of two priests, two missionary nuns, and Simone. It served an area with 60,000 Indian and 200 non-Indian inhabitants. The older priest, Padre Ramon, tended to the church in Tecpan's center, while Father Mike dealt with a corps of Indian catechists who said the rosary in the hamlets. The nuns, Sister Paula Marie and Sister Patricia, ran a clinic for the Indians. Sister Paula was trained as a public health nurse, and Sister Patricia "just helped out". Paula Marie says she's not good for much more than praying over the terminal cases, but the Indians love her. There are already several rumors of miracles she's accomplished in bringing the dead back to life. I tell her she's the one that will end up as a saint, or at least beatified, whole Sister Paula Marie is still in purgatory for her impure thoughts."

This last was enough to arouse Father Mike, and he interjected, "Now Simone…"

"Well, why does she always insist on doing physical exams on the twelve-year-old boys in the public school? Even the peasants from the far hamlets are beginning to talk. Padre Ramon says the mayor came over last week to ask about it. The mayor claims that after she does her hernia check, the boys can't play *futbol* for a week. I swear, the only words she knows in Mayan are "turn your head and cough.""

"Sister Paula Marie has done a great deal of good in the years that she's been here," Father Mike began.

"So, if she wants to feel up a few preadolescent children, what's the harm?" Simone continued his sentence. "Maybe you're right. Maybe that's why Pedro Daniel keeps flunking fifth grade. If he's in love with her, he's in for a big disappointment." She paused to correct herself. "It's your pants she wants to get into, not his."

"Simone!" Father Mike's voice was almost a shout. Then, in a more conversational tone, he addressed me as if she weren't present. "You'll have to learn to ignore most of what Simone tells you, Mister Fletcher. She loves to say provocative things."

"I'll bet every word of it is true," I said, hoping that a jocular tone would ease the situation, though my words sounded lame even to my ears.

"Out of the mouths of babes," said Simone.

"Where do we turn off for Tecpan?" I asked to change the subject. We'd been coasting along through the afternoon and I hadn't given much thought to our route. Now the gas was below a quarter tank and I had the impression Father Mike was so unworldly that he'd let us run right by our turn off without saying a word.

"There's a gasoline station in Chimaltenango," he said. "If you want, we could get some food from the restaurant next door. After that it's just fifty kilometers straight on the Panamerican highway. You can't miss Tecpan. It's just before you get to the next range of mountains."

We stopped at the *gasolinera* and picked up a couple of beers, but they didn't have any that were cold. Simone bought a half dozen little tamales from a woman sitting by one of the pumps, but the taste was so acrid that I pitched mine into the ditch once we were clear of town.

"Litter bug," said Simone.

"It's biodegradable," I said. In 1970, the word was new and impressive. The first Earth Day was yet to be held, but in a biology department we'd been using it for years.

"Shut up, Jim," said Simone, "or you'll make me fall out of love with you."

"I take a vow of silence," I replied. "For your love, I would do anything, for your precious love."

"Don't take the name of Percy Sledge in vain," said Simone.

"Percy Sledge didn't sing *For Your Precious Love*."

"Sure he did."

"It couldn't have been Percy Sledge."

"Well, who did, then?"

"I can't think of it right now, but it wasn't Percy Sledge."

We blithered on, but the work "love" had been spoken. It reverberated in the cab without making a sound, and, hanging there, began to affect everything that would be said or done. It promised earthly delight; it bound us together. Father Mike relapsed into silence, and I wondered whether Simone's verbal play had been too rough for him, leaving him sullen and withdrawn. Or had love had its impact on him too? If I took what Simone said seriously, he also was the object of illicit desire.

Father Mike was the first priest I'd ever spoken with, and like most unreligious people, the fact of his celibacy was hard for me to understand. To me, priests were people who showed up on convention platforms dressed in a strange collar to deliver invocations, or who served as the butt of priest-rabbi jokes. Looking at him, I felt like a child who turned on the television set late Christmas morning to find *Truth or Consequences* or *The Price is Right* babbling along just as if were an ordinary day, when everything else about that morning was so different. The fact that Bob Barker was wearing a Santa hat did nothing to lessen the inappropriateness. So too, our banter, the first halting steps of a game that would result in physical consummation seemed out of place next to Father Mike, who could never experience the joy of intercourse.

Uncomfortable as I was in the truck, I didn't look forward to our arrival in Tecpan. If Father Mike made me feel ill at ease, what would the presence of a second priest and a pair of nuns do? For all of my illusions in the *El Vaquero,* I was hardly a Don Juan prepared to scale Simone's balcony and ravish her despite the watchful guard of her duenna. I was not searching for a conquest. What I wanted from Simone was both pure and physical. I wanted her with a freshness deriving from my long isolation. As the low ridge of mountains marking the end of the plateau appeared before us, I struggled to find what to say next. One could hardly rent a room in an Indian town as you would check into a motel in the United States. Still, there had been no mention of my staying at the mission. Gingerly, I looked for an opening.

"Would there be somewhere I could crash at the mission for the night?" I asked, hoping that my approach would not look too hang dog.

It was Father Mike's turn to stare. "Well, you can't go on after dark. If the guerillas don't take a pot shot at you, the army will."

"Well, I mean..." I began.

"Of course you'll stay. I'll just ask Maria to dust off one of the guest rooms. The mission's so enormous we just rattle around in there. We inherited from the Germans, and they're terrific builders. They had a lay brother who was a mason and the man just kept adding rooms. They get tax money, you know."

"No, I didn't know."

"Oh, the Germans are loaded with cash. They only thing they aren't good at is dealing with the Indians. They keep trying to stamp out idolatry. They absolutely freak out if the Indian brotherhood wants to have the shaman put a prayer to the spirit in the mountain somewhere in the middle of the mass."

"And you don't mind?" I led.

"It's their own form of Catholicism. The church has always made its peace with pagan practices. Where do you think Easter eggs and Easter bunnies come from? Pagan fertility symbols."

'That seems pretty open-minded," I said, not quite knowing what to say.

"Father Ramon had enormous trouble in his first years. The native brotherhoods had been fighting with the priest for so long, it had become a habit. On the other hand, if you follow the Germans you certainly get first-class accommodations."

"You should see the plumbing system they set up," said Simone. "The mission has its own well, a diesel generator for when the power goes down, bottle gas water heaters, and a septic tank that never backs up. Oh look, there's Tecpan now."

Tecpan looked like every other Indian town I'd seen – adobe houses on a checkerboard of dirt streets, the irregular roofs of a few market stalls in the plaza, and a colonial church with a cheap and rusted metal roof.

We turned off the highway, lurched across a concrete bridge, and rolled up to the church, leaving the street urchins coughing in the dust of our passage. Simone and Father Mike crossed themselves as I drifted to a halt past the doorway.

"Why don't I show Jim the town while you tell Maria to set another place for dinner," said Simone.

"Should I leave the truck here at the square?" I asked.

"You can for now," said Father Mike, opening the door and hopping out. "We'll open the back gate and let you park in the mission courtyard tonight. Best not to leave anything unguarded."

He walked up the two worn stone steps and in through the doorway of the church, leaving Simone and me sitting in the truck with her leg still pressed against mine. Abruptly she slid across the seat and out the door.

"Better lock it up," she said, slamming the door.

By the time I'd rolled up the windows, she was halfway across the plaza. I was uncertain whether to race to her side or simply let my somewhat faster walk overtake her, so I loped awkwardly between the two paces until we reached the far side of the square simultaneously. She linked her arm in mine and we headed down a potholed street toward the edge of town.

"I wanted to talk to you in private," she said. "Padre Ramon is a great guy, but I don't think he'd understand if he found you in my room tonight. It would be better if I came to yours. That way you won't blunder in on anyone else."

"OK." I barely breathed the word in an effort to sound unsurprised.

"You don't think I'm too forward, do you?" she asked. "After all, it's only Guatemala." Now, what did that mean?

"Oh, no," I said. "But don't you think I should kiss you first?"

"Silly," she said. "Not here. People just wouldn't understand. I mean, I hope you don't mind sneaking around like this. It's not as if we're doing anything wrong."

"Oh, no. Nothing wrong."

"I knew you'd understand," she said and squeezed my arm. We had reached the edge of the village and looked out over a swale of pasture toward the mountains. The breeze blew Simone's hair against my neck, and I felt the greatest sense of peace and anticipation I have encountered in my lifetime.

CHAPTER 4

It had been easy to recognize Simone's busy chatter in the Scout as an introduction to the society I would find in the mission at Tecpan. Father Mike's mention of the German builder was equally an attempt at softening the shock as we I walked into the rectory behind the church. From the street, the mission's adobe walls looked indistinguishable from those around them. Once inside, I might have been standing in the lobby of a Bavarian inn. The ceiling of the entry hall rose sharply overhead, the floor was laid in wide, softwood boards (some split by the humidity of the rainy season), and at the far end yawned the biggest fireplace I'd ever seen – a monster done in gray stone with an elevated hearth. Apparently, the fireplace did not draw too well, for the beam of the mantel bore traces of escaped smoke. The room was as gloomy as a Teutonic mead hall.

"It's amazing," I said.

"Wait until you see the dining room," said Simone. "It makes you want to roll out maps on the table and plan the summer campaign for the Eastern Front." She pulled me after her like a girl showing her father around summer camp.

The dining room was as big as the entry hall, but lighter and easier to take. One whole wall consisted of glass doors opening onto the patio. The table, big enough to seat eighteen people, must have weighed 600 pounds. Four enormous pedestals arranged down the central axis supported a slap of polished mahogany that reflected blurred images of the patio outside. Five place settings were grouped at one end and a heavy-set, dark-skinned woman was in the process of laying a sixth place – mine, I presumed.

"Maria," said Simone, continuing to pull me along, "*Este es Jeem*."

"*Mucho gusto, Señor,*" said Maria.

"Maria came with the mission," explained Simone. "The Germans trained her, so of course she's very big on titles. She's never forgiven us our American ways."

"*Mucho gusto, Doña Maria,*" I said, holding out my hand. Maria turned on her heel and bustled from the room.

"She hates it when people come in just before dinner. At least you're not one of Father Mike's catechists. She stares at them while she serves, as if they had no right to be there."

"Isn't Maria an Indian too?" "Maria would go nuts if she heard you say that. She must tell me her father was pure Ladino twice a week."

"Does she ever eat with you?" "No. Padre Ramon tried before anyone else was here, but she wouldn't have it. She doesn't like the fact we eat at six o'clock either, but you'd better be prompt. I guess the Germans ate much later. At 6:15, she snatches the food back and makes you eat in the kitchen if you arrive later, just for spite."

"Who runs this place, her or you?"

"Oh, you'll never get Maria to change. We just go along with her. We've only got twenty minutes until

dinner, so you'd better wash up. I'll show you your
room."

The hallway was the first clue that the opulence
of the mission was confined to its public spaces. The
cement floor and whitewashed walls led down a corridor
with doorways as regularly spaced as the rooms in a
motel. Each plain wooden door had a wrought iron
latch. The lintels were so low I had to stoop to get
through. The only window in my room was a narrow slit
with frosted glass that suffused the interior with an
anemic glow.

The furnishings were sparse – a bureau, a mirror,
and a plain wooden bed with a foam rubber mattress. A
crucifix hung from a nail in the wall above the bed. The
facing wall held the doorway to a bathroom the size of a
closet. Simone bounced on the bed and patted the
mattress with affection.

"Not much give in these. Padre Ramon says they
are orthopedically correct, which is why he sent to
Cleveland for a Sealy that wasn't."

"I've got no complaints," I said. I felt awkward.
It felt as if the ghost of the departed German priest still
inhabited the room, guarding against any deviation from
celibacy on the premises.

Simone stood up as suddenly as she had plopped
down on the bed and put her arms around me. "One kiss
before dinner," she announced. "If we make out too
long, my lips will be red and I'll feel self-conscious."

She put her arms around me, and as our lips met
and parted, I felt her tongue's first gentle exploration. I
pulled her as tight to me as I could. The kiss went on
and on, neither of us wanting to offend the other by

pulling away. She was so slender that my arms cradled her to me. If the ghost of the German priest saw that kiss, he could just as well eat his heart out. I knew I would never be shy about what was going to happen.

In the end it was Simone who pulled away. "I'll get some towels and leave them outside the door. You could use a shower."

A heater powered by bottled gas provided the hot water. After three explosive bursts of air trapped in the line, the head produced a sumptuous rush of steaming water, turning my chest bright red where it caught the force of the flow. The plumbing gave a comforting roar as the steam billowed in the narrow cavity of the bathroom and the water gurgled down the drain. I lathered and rinsed over and over, feeling lusciously clean for the first time since my arrival in Guatemala.

Suddenly it occurred to me that I had lost all track of time. I bolted into the bedroom, skidding on the cement floor and clutching at the headboard to keep from falling. I swiped the towel across my body a few times. I whispered curses as my shirt clung to my back and my socks refused to slide over my heels. Frantic wiping at the mirror finally freed a spot so I could part my hair, and I clumped back into the dining room only a minute and a half after six. Maria's malevolent glance bounded off my clean, rejuvenated exterior. I slid into the only empty chair, the one beside Simone, with perfunctory apologies for my tardiness.

"Everybody, this is Jim," said Simone brightly. "I brought him along to be the token Protestant for the mission. If you feed him a cracker, he will utter ecumenical phrases." Had she practiced the line while I was showering?

"Pleased to meet you, Jim," said Padre Ramon, whose obesity and balding head gave him a Friar Tuck look that his tent of a Hawaiian shirt could not completely erase. "J know you've met Mike, so I'll just introduce Sister Patricia and Sister Paula Marie."

"Simone has told me a lot about you," I said, and regretted it as I saw Father Mike shift in his chair.

Sister Patricia looked as if she had been washed far too thoroughly as a child and never recovered. Her hair was pale yellow, her complexion coarse and white. Though her features were ordinary enough, they seemed to hang on her face in awkward disarray, and the nervous smile she shot in my direction was tentative and uneven. Having looked up, she dropped her eyes once again to her plate.

Sister Paula Marie, while no better looking, had a pleasant middle-aged air about her and met my gaze directly. She had pulled her dark hair back in to a bun, but the pleasant roundness of her cheeks kept her from looking severe. Like Sister Patricia she wore no cosmetics, but on her businesslike features the absence seemed appropriate. "I wouldn't believe everything Simone says," she said in an even tone, "She lives in a far more dramatic world than the rest of us."

"I object," said Simone. "I may not agree with what you say, but I will defend to the death my right to be as pedestrian as the rest of you."

Maria plopped back into the room carrying an enormous willowware tureen, made of the kind of cheap China you see at a dollar store. She placed it in front of

Padre Ramon. He lifted the lid, sniffed the steam, and began to ladle the soup into the bowls stacked by his place. By the time my bowl reached me, Maria had returned with a plate on which she had stacked saltines. The liquid before me was a clear broth in which sliced vegetables swam accompanied by an all too easily identified chicken heart.

"Maria's cooking is this mission's approach to mortification of the flesh." Padre Ramon's voice boomed down the table.

"After nothing but eggs and beans for a month, anything looks good," I said. "I mean, I'm sure it will be wonderful," I added, for fear of sounding ungrateful.

"Well, there's no three-bite rule at this table," said Simone, pushing her bowl away. "My advice is to wait for the tortillas. She buys them from a woman in the market."

I dipped my spoon into the broth and took a tentative sip. I knew it was my obligation as a guest to clean my plate. Maria had managed to eliminate all the flavor from the vegetables without leaving any trace in the surrounding broth. As a result, only the acrid taste of the giblets remained, omnipresent and unavoidable, like God, pervading broth and vegetable alike. Compelled by the training of a thousand childhood mealtimes, I dipped my spoon for a second time. The table burst into laughter.

"I told you he was sweet," Simone said to Padre Ramon. "Sweet" again.

"You should have kept quiet," he replied. "The way he went back so quickly, there is a good chance he would have broken the record."

"What record?" I asked.

"We once had an anthropologist who actually downed five spoonfuls of Maria's soup," said Padre Ramon. "He was suffering from dysentery which, in my opinion, had killed his sense of taste. Nobody eats Maria's soup. It's just a way of beginning the meal."

I had survived some rite of passage with the second spoonful, even though I never got it to my lips. It was ritual marked not by humiliation or torture of the subject, but by a subconscious test of his character.

"How was the city?" asked Padre Ramon.

"A most disturbing trip," said Father Mike. "On the way back, we saw a boy being tortured by the National Police."

"Guats," snorted Padre Ramon. "I'm not surprised by anything they do."

"I'm as much disturbed at my own behavior as theirs," said Father Mike. "We saw him being pulled from the car and taken into a shack, we heard his cries for help, and I just drove on."

"What could you do about it?" asked Padre Ramon.

"I just have the feeling we should have done something," Father Mike answered, looking down at the tablecloth. "I guess I've always known how brutal the police can be, but to actually see someone be dragged away..."

"Tell Jim about the incident you saw at Patzicia," said Simone.

Padre Ramon stopped carving a chicken that Maria placed before him and for the first time I saw the comfortable complaisance leave him. "I was at the fiesta

in Patzicia," he began. "Some soldiers were there –
drunk, of course, swaggering down a side street. One of
the Indians wouldn't get out of the way for them. So, the
soldier took his machine gun and fired a burst right into
the crowd. Three people were killed just as I came
around the corner. One bled out right at my feet. And
do you know how the newspapers reported it? An Indian
riot put down by the forces of order!"

"That's terrible," I said.

Padre Ramon sat back like a frog settling on a
lily pad. "Guats," he grunted. "Do you know why all
the missions in Guatemala are run by foreign priests?"

"I didn't know they were," I said.

"Because the Guat priests refuse to serve in the
countryside. There are 130 native Guatemalan priests,
and 110 of them are in Guatemala City. They didn't
become priests to associate with Indians. They all figure
they've earned the bright lights of the capital." He
hacked a leg from the chicken and passed it to Sister
Patricia.

"I've decided to make a formal complaint," said
Father Mike. "If we do not speak up on these issues,
then who will? To permit this kind of thing to happen
and maintain silence is to become an accomplice in it."

"Who are you going to complain to?" I asked.
"It seems to me a government which didn't object to its
citizens being gunned down in the streets isn't going to
be bothered by a letter of complaint."
As I spoke, I saw a frown cross Simone's face. It
brought me up short. Had I revealed a fundamentally
un-sweet side of my nature? Would I spend the night

alone in my room, wishing I'd learned to keep my mouth shut?

"That doesn't matter," said Father Mike. "Whether or not our protests are effective, there is a moral responsibility to speak out. Otherwise we're just like the good Germans who let Hitler slaughter the Jews."

People talked that way in the '70s.

"All Jim is saying," said Simone, "is that you have to think carefully before you act. I mean a futile gesture might be worse than none at all."

"Exactly," I said, feeling a physical thrill of anticipation with the thought Simone might still be within my grasp. This was not time to bring up the possibility Father Mike could be getting himself and the mission in a shitload of trouble.

Still, no matter how amoral I might pride myself on being, there was still residual guilt about my willingness to trade everyone at the table for a shot at Simone's body. As I was speaking, I could feel my eyes drop. Not wanting to appear shifty-eyed, I raised them and found myself looking directly across the table at Sister Patricia.

She wasn't looking at me. It was my guilt that made me think anyone was. Her eyes were on Father Mike, bathing him in rapt adulation as a mother might gaze upon an only son who was distinguishing himself at an elementary school recital. It was a look of total, unquestioning approval – benign, loving, serene.

"Patricia, if you don't take this plate my arm's going to drop off," grunted Padre Ramon, holding out her portion to her. She looked flustered and began to blush.

"I guess I was just thinking about what Mike said," she mumbled, though there was no need to explain.

"Carried away by the sweep of his theology," snickered Simone.

"I was wondering how many people are going to join me in a hot game of Risk," said Padre Ramon. "It is my contention that control of Irkutsk and Yakutsk are the key. If you put major armies there, you'll end up controlling Asia, and once you get Asia's seven bonus armies each turn, you're in like Flynn."

'I haven't played Risk in years," I said.

"I like Argentina the best," said Simone. "As long as you control Brazil and Peru, nobody can attack you. And since South America is only worth two armies, the gringos quickly overrun you and you can go to bed early."

I knew a hint when I heard it. "I'll take Southern Europe, get squeezed between Africa and the Germans, and be done in no time."

"Nothing for me tonight," said Father Mike. "I'm going to start drafting my letter to the American ambassador."

"Risk's no good without at least five players," grumped Padre Ramon. "The deal-making is too limited."

Maria plopped back into the room and the table fell silent again. I later found out Padre Ramon thought it rude to speak English when anyone in the room couldn't understand what was being said. For me, one of the advantages of traveling in Guatemala was the sense I'd been endowed with a secret code giving me the freedom to comment bluntly upon the surrounding scene. Even among Guatemalans who spoke English fluently, it was no problem to slip into slang or make allusions to long dead situation comedies. At the table, we deferred to Padre Ramon's sensibilities.

It is hard to tell, after all this time, exactly what is remembered and what has been interpolated with later experience and projected back into my first evening at the mission, but I think I realized as I sat there, that the mission had constructed a family in that far country. Ramon was the benevolent father – knowing, trustworthy, and secure. Father Mike was the eldest son, youthful and ambitious, idolized by his sisters. Simone was the baby, indulged and spoiled, prized for the diversion her pranks and tantrums provided. I was the boyfriend, a figure to be entertained and examined – an alien, dependent and immature, but endowed with the power to break the bonds of kinship and spirit away the family prize.

The mother of this family (and here I am clearly adding my later intuitions) was the church itself. It was the church that had assembled the household. They were called by the offer to love them eternally, as a mother loves, no matter what they looked like, no matter what their failings. They were refugees from their own society – wallflowers at school dances, the boys who never appreciated the smutty confidences of the locker room.   The church adopted them and made them her own. Mother Church wrapped them in the redeeming love of Jesus Christ and set them about their chores.

They, in turn, loved her back, shared the eccentricities of belief, as children, loving, are embarrassed by the foibles of their parents even as they come to mirror them in turn.

Some of these ideas I saw clearly then, some I sensed, and some I have written back into the past. Then I thought Simone was different from the others at the mission. I was like a man who won a Rolls Royce on a quiz show, overwhelmed by the magnitude of my good fortune, but unprepared to face the costs and responsibilities of possession. Least of all was I inclined to question the events which had so endowed me, to wonder why a nineteen-year-old girl, who might otherwise be enjoying her freshman year in college had chosen to spend her time in a far land accompanied by strangers. I was content to accept Simone's presence as a caprice, and believe, with the innocence of the young, that the universe had bestowed upon me its greatest prize, simply for the effort of reaching out to take it.

CHAPTER 5

Dessert was an agony of anticipation accompanied by flan, the tasteless custard that seems to end even the best Guatemalan meals. Padre Ramon, unable to interest either Patricia or Paula Marie in Risk, sulked at the head of the table. Father Mike sat quietly. Occasionally his lips moved, trying out the phrases he must have been composing in his head. Patricia and Paula Marie got into a conversation about the medicines they needed for the clinic. Simone worked her way to the bottom of her bowl without enthusiasm. During our meal, hurried as it was, the short tropical sunset had passed, turning the glass doors beside the table into mirrors that reflected out glum company back upon itself.

"Let's go for a walk," said Simone. "The company around here is too senile."

"You don't have to use us as an excuse for walking with your *novio,*" said Padre Ramon. "Wandering about under the moon. Very romantic, I would say."

"There's a moon out tonight, let's go a strollin'," sang Father Mike in a tuneless falsetto.

"It's better than sitting here playing Risk," Simone retorted.

"Don't do anything I wouldn't do," chortled Padre Ramon. "And remember, it's just as easy to love a rich man."

I stood up with Simone and sidled toward the hall. I longed for some zippy comeback and was unable to come up with any sort of repartee. Simone seemed similarly taken aback, so we walked through the doorway together.

"They're just trying to be funny," said Simone.

"Well, I want to see the town by moonlight," I said. "Tomorrow the moon is full, so it should already be above the horizon. It will look enormous."

"You really know about that stuff, don't you?" said Simone. Was there admiration in her voice?

"Know about it? I have to enter the phase of the moon on every goddamn moth I collect. If I knew more about the moon, I'd probably rise and fall, like the tides. You'd have to scrape me off the ceiling with every spring tide."

"You have to scrape me off the ceiling in the spring, too."

I started to explain her error, but I caught the words and held them back. I needed that mistake in her, and not telling her about it kept her a little more fascinating because it made her less perfect. I opened the door to the street for her, the kind of courtesy that could get you in trouble in those early days of women's liberation, and she walked through without affectation.

We stopped at a store on the square, really just the front room of someone's home equipped with a painted wooden counter and a refrigerator, to buy a couple of beers and a pack of Belmont cigarettes. The square boasted a pair of chipped concrete benches, a waterless fountain, and a dispirited mock orange bush. Even though it wasn't yet seven, the streets were empty, and every window shuttered. Snatches of marimba music from radios set out on patios floated over the tile roofs. With no streetlights for competition, the moon washed the village with pale alchemy, turning dusty roads into silver highways and the adobe walls into a cubist's dream.

"I hope you didn't get the wrong idea from our conversation in the El Vaquero," said Simone. "I really didn't sleep around all that much in high school. I don't want you to think I was the town slut."

"Don't say that. You're destroying my illusions."

"I mean, it's not like I'm a virgin or anything," she continued, artlessly.

"I don't think God cares about stuff like that." Was she turning religious on me? I was struck by the fear last minute scruples were going to rob me of my prize. It wasn't fair. I had been cheerful and friendly and eaten my dinner like a good boy. It would be an enormous injustice if she were to rediscover a primitive sense of morality.

"God cares," she said. "But I think he understands. After all, he knocked up the BVM, didn't he?"

"The BVM?"

"Blessed Virgin Mary," she said, as if explaining something to a kindergartener.

"I never thought of Mary as the high school cheerleader who come across for the Great Quarterback in the Sky."

"I don't know if it was intercourse," she said, "but it was certainly premarital."

"Did the nuns teach you that?"

"Oh, no. The nuns taught health and hygiene, not religion. And the priest who did the New Testament didn't slow down enough to allow any questions at that point. He could hardly wait for the crucifixion."

"I can hardly wait either," I said and put an arm around her. The more Simone talked about sex, the more innocent she appeared to me. The moonlight made her look even younger than she had that first moment at the El Vaquero.

"I mean, all that talk about Protestant boys," she went on. "There was only one Protestant boy and we'd gone together for a year before we made love. I think I liked sneaking away to see Tommy as much as I liked him. You know how it is when you are a kid."

It was hard not to laugh at that. Her dates with Tommy couldn't have occurred more than a year ago.

"Where's Tommy now?" I asked.

"In the army someplace," she said with a gesture of impatience. "I was so pissed off at him. He had to go flunk out of Penn State just to get back at his mother. It isn't easy to flunk out of Penn State. You really have to work at it."

"Do you write to him?"

"Not since we broke up, almost a year ago. You know how it is."

I didn't know how it was, but I said, "Sure, I know."

"What about you?" she asked, and I realized she was carrying me toward the brink of intimacy. After all, if you're going to bed with someone, you have to take off your clothes. By telling me about Tommy, Simone was coercing me into a similar set of revelations.

"What about me?" I countered.

"Come on. I showed you mine, now you've got to show me yours."

"Well, I was living with a woman at Berkeley before I came down here, but it wasn't working out."

"Did she cheat on you? Was she frigid? Maybe you tried to make her serve you breakfast in bed every morning wearing nothing but an apron and high heels."

"Nothing that exciting. We got bored with each other."

"And here I thought that you'd be so great in bed that I'd be your love slave for life."

"Naw, I got tired of love slaves by the time Gretchen came along. Hey, it looks like he's closing the store. Let's get a couple more beers before the place shuts down."

The owner had appeared in the lighted doorway, looking into the vacant plaza before closing the door. I dashed across to him, driven by the need to escape Simone's confessional mood, and returned with two warm bottles of Gallo and a half dozen little packages of Tor-Trix, barbecue flavored corn chips. By the time I got back, Simone had lit another Belmont and was staring at the moon.

"What did you mean when you said that God doesn't care if people sleep together?" she asked.

"I mean even if there's a God, the universe is so enormous that it just doesn't matter what any one person does." Back to God again. This didn't look good.

"I think God cares, but he's basically a nice guy," said Simone. "He's looking down right now and saying, 'Have a good time.'"

"What church did you say you go to?" I asked.

"Oh, you'll never find God in church," she said, as if stating the most obvious fact in the world. "Rip open another bag of those Tor-Trix."

We stayed in the park for an hour, trying to make our beers last and jabbering about whatever popped into our brains. I lay on the bench with my head in her lap. When she leaned over to kiss me her face was in shadow and the moonlight made a luminescent halo of her hair. I reached up to touch her breast, the first gentle intrusion of the night's promised intimacy, and when she kissed me again, she stroked my cheek. All the doubts of the day's anticipation slipped away, and I was rocked in the warm certainty of the night to come.

"Everybody will be in bed by nine," said Simone. "I'll come down to your room by nine-thirty. Don't fall asleep waiting."

Not much chance of that.

When we got back to the mission, Padre Ramon sat alone at the table in the dining room, working his way through a solemn hand of solitaire.

"The black five will go on the red six," said Simone, leaning over his shoulder.

"Yes," he said, "but I'm afraid that's it. One more card to turn over and only seven cards up on the aces. If I had the two of diamonds, I could put up the three, four, and five." He turned over the last card, the nine of clubs. "And that won't go anywhere," he said sweeping the cards into a pile.

"I can never play solitaire," said Simone. "I always cheat."

"But then there's no joy in winning," he answered. "I mean there's no surprise if things always turn out right. The pleasure of solitaire is that one wins so seldom."

"I intend," said Simone, "to spend my days going from one great moment of fulfillment to another without any intervening sadness. Good night, Jim." She winked at me behind Padre Ramon's back and left the room.

"I guess I better be turning in as well," I said.

"Jim?" said Padre Ramon. It was more an order to stay than a question.

I stopped at the doorway.

"I'm glad Simone met you in the city. I'm afraid that we're pretty dreary company at times out here."

"Oh, no," I said, "All she could talk about on the drive over here in the Scout was the people of the mission. You're like a little world to her."

He looked as if he were going to say something significant, halted, and then just said, "Good night, Jim."

I turned from the lighted dining room into the darkened hall, fumbling through my mind to remember which door was mine. Third on the right, I thought. The second door showed a crack of light at the floor with the sound of a typewriter leaking into the hall. Apparently, Father Mike was putting his mental composition at the dinner table into tangible form. I opened the door I thought was mine, groped for the light switch, and sighed with relief. It wouldn't do to surprise Sister Patricia in the middle of her nunly toilette.

Simone arrived promptly at nine-thirty, as if she were on time for an appointment with an ophthalmologist. She opened the door and slipped in without knocking, easing it back to the jamb and releasing the latch so there wasn't any click.

"This is great," she said. "Padre Kohl and Father Mike are both still awake, one typing, the other probably praying. And we're in here..." She let the sentence drift away, searching for the proper verb.

She was wearing a cotton nightgown, plain, almost girlish in cut, but on the figure, I'd ogled at the El Vaquero nothing could look too girlish. She had pulled her hair back into a ponytail. I'd jumped up from the bed when she appeared, and I took a step over to her. After a great deal of thought over the last half hour, I'd decided to wear only what I would be expected to have on has someone else come in, in this case, my underwear.

"Jockey shorts," she said. "Most becoming."

"Shut up," I said. "What did you expect? That I'd swing in nude, like Tarzan, shouting 'the vine, Jane, the vine!'"

"What?"

"An old joke. Never mind."

It was not a time for talk. I told myself to go slow, because lonely as I was, I could have mounted her in fifteen seconds and found relief. I kissed her for a long time with a lot of tongue, and she pulled me against her so hard I felt the breath go out of my lungs.

Simone hadn't lied when she said she was no virgin. She knew what she was looking for. There was no tentative exploration, but a search for something wanted not because it is strange, but because it is familiar, elemental, and necessary. She ran her hands up my back to my shoulder blades, her fingers firm but gentle. My hands reached past the curve of her buttocks and stroked the backs of her thighs.

It was a dream to me. That morning I had been desperate and alone, and now here she was. Each caress was special because it reassured me that she was real, she was in my arms, and she was about to give herself to me, freely and completely, not seduced or manipulated, but because she longed to be in bed with someone (anyone?) as much as I did.

She tweaked my butt as we let go of one another and bounced onto the bed. "Last one to have an orgasm's a rotten egg," she announced.

"Don't be like that," I said.

"You're not going soft on me, getting mushy?"

"Don't worry," I said. "It's hard as a rock."

"No, I meant you aren't going to be all romantic, like a tourist."

"I just meant shut up," I said and pulled her against me.

"Let me get my night gown off," she said, and pulled it up over her head with a single flowing motion. "Smooth, huh?" she said. "Eight years of ballet lessons."

"Damn," I said, struggling to push my underwear down my legs.

"Shh," she said, and I heard the slap of Padre Ramon's *huaraches* coming down the corridor. I put my arms around her and we both struggled to control our giggles as the steps approached, then proceeded reassuringly on down the hallway.

"Now," I whispered. "We've got to do it while he's still awake. Otherwise the danger of getting caught will be gone."

She put her arms around me and pulled me down on top of her. Our bodies were firm and young and alive, and I felt her body stretched against mine. The longing that had never left me since the El Vaquero overwhelmed me, and as I stroked her body, my every nerve seemed to extend beyond the boundary of my skin. Then I knew that I could take it very, very slow indeed and not let this moment fade. I would take the time to enjoy her and know that she was enjoying me. When I could wait no longer, I reached for the condom I had secreted on the bed stand even before undressing.

"Thank you," whispered Simone as I fumbled to unroll it.

"I love you," I whispered back, because she had startled me and I couldn't think of anything else to say. There was no time for explanations and, as I entered her and she arched her body to accept me, the words were swept away. In the desperate silence as we ground our way to that ecstatic, shuddering release, it seemed as if everything we had said had been wiped clean, the way the surf polishes a beach in a rising tide. And yet, nothing was lost, for the words come back to me as clearly now as the recollection of desire, and the memory of those urgent whispers in the darkness, is as clear as the sensation of that wonderful, involuntary climax that we shared.

*   *   *   *   *   *   *

63

I lay awake long past midnight, with Simone crammed up against me on the narrow mattress. I felt warm, clean, and satisfied, intoxicated with my incredibly good fortune, letting the images of the day wash back through my mind, and feeling young and elegant, adventurous and in love. The longings of so extended a period of deprivation were far from spent in that single act, and as I lay in the darkness, the curves of Simone's body, half seen half felt, my penis once again became erect, stirring with a life of its own, producing the pleasant promise of desire reawakened combined with the certainty that it would be slaked once again.

Still, something beyond my need for Simone was keeping me from sleep – some submerged discontent swam in my unconscious, rippling the surface with an odd, unfocussed threat to my happiness. Drowsy, half amused, I let my mind wander back through the day, the trip, the meeting at the El Vaquero.

It was the letter from MacElwain. I snapped awake. It must be there in my backpack beside the bed, as it had been since it appeared maliciously in the postal box in the capital city that morning. "I'll read it tomorrow," I thought, and struggled to reestablish that satiated sense of peace that surrounded the two of us on the bed. It was no use, the letter had worked its evil magic, and I knew I couldn't sleep until it was read.

I slipped my arm from around Simone and snapped on the light on the shelf that served as a bedside table. She didn't stir as the light came on, though it was bright enough to make spots hover in front of my eyes. My backpack was under the shelf, an easy stretch. I fumbled the buckle open.

The letter was typed, as all MacElwain's letters were, on plain cotton bond by a manual machine in desperate need of cleaning.

February 23
Dear Jim
I received the carbon copy of your last set of observations only a week ago and have taken the time to review the overall thrust of your data as a way of ensuring that the research meets the standards of most rigorous criticism when it is finally published. It is difficult to describe the sense of excitement that I felt when my preliminary analysis was complete. You may well have collected the evidence that totally obliterates any lingering doubts that seasonality is a function of temperature in tropical moths. The struggle to convince the scientific establishment that thermal determinism is the single, elegant explanation for the cycles of all moths in whatever climate has been a difficult one, but together we may soon enjoy the fruits of success.

I noticed with dismay, however, that a number of your observations obscure the fundamental pattern, and I am certain these results are caused by sloppiness in observation, particularly with respect to the lunar cycle. It is essential that you take especial care not to miss any nights within four days of the full moon in each of the coming months to eliminate this error from your data. I realize that this work can be fatiguing at times, but without the utmost rigor it might be impossible to defend your thesis against critics within the department who could make getting your degree problematic in the extreme.

Just like MacElwain, I thought - an indirect threat to hold my degree hostage if I didn't support his approach.

In order to be certain that no mistakes enter the material at this late date, I have arranged to fly to Guatemala to visit your field site. I'll arrive on the afternoon flight from Los Angeles on March 28. You can make reservations for me at the Panamerican Hotel in Guatemala City.

Looking forward to seeing you then,

Robert MacElwain
(How typical of MacElwain to use his full name)
"Oh, shit," I said, aloud, and dropped the letter to the floor.

CHAPTER 6

"I'll invade Afghanistan from China with three armies," said Padre Ramon. "You can only defend with one."

"My sturdy Afghan mocks your Oriental hordes," I said, rolling a five. Kohl rolled a two, three, and six.

"Afghanistan falls," he chortled, picking up my army and discarding it. "Now I'll invade India from China with three armies. You can only defend with your one."

"If India falls, what have you got left, Jim?" asked Simone, making no attempt to disguise the boredom in her voice.

"Just Scandinavia and Quebec," I said. and rolled a six. "Down you go, Ramon."

"I'll attack India with three armies again," he said, replacing his fallen armies from a pile that spread from the Himalayas to the Yellow Sea. All of Asia will be mine. I told you Irkutsk was the key."

"You told us that Sunday night, Wednesday night, and Thursday night," said Simone. "At Mass, I thought I heard you say, 'Irkutsk is the key to Asia' as you elevated the host."

Padre chuckled good-naturedly as his armies reached the Bay of Bengal.

"I'm ready to make a treaty, Mike," I said. "I'll give you Scandinavia and Quebec, if you'll give me the last cookie on the plate."

"And I'll give Mike Central America, Argentina, and East Africa," Simone chimed in. "That way you'll have all of North America, South America, and Africa. Ten armies at the start of each turn."

"What will I give you in exchange?" Father Mike asked.

"Oh, I'll have Jim's cookie," she said.

"Sounds like a deal to me," I said, grabbing the cookie and heading for the door.

"This is desertion in time of war," Padre Ramon shouted after us. "I'll have you hung from the yard arm. I'll have you keel-hauled."

"They only do that in the navy," Simone called over her shoulder. "We're army brats."

Whatever Padre Ramon had to say to that was cut short by the slam of the front door of the mission behind us as we exited. The inertia of our mad dash across the entry hall carried us into the middle of the street, and we pulled up laughing and triumphant in the cool night air.

"Do you think he'll be mad we ditched?" I asked, not really caring what the answer might be.

"He doesn't really care," she answered. "I'll smooth it over to him tomorrow when I go into confession."

"You're going to confession tomorrow?" The idea of what else Simone would have to confess to brought me up short.

"Of course. If you don't go to confession, you can't accept the host. You've got to be in a state of grace."

"Does that mean that you're going to tell him about us sleeping together?"

"I'm not going to tell him; I'm going to confess it. There's all the difference in the world."

"Oh, sweet Jesus," I said, the slap of Padre Ramon's _huaraches_ down the hall echoing in my mind. "Couldn't you just wait and confess to some Guatemalan priest next time you go to the capital?"

"What's the big deal?" she asked. "When you go into the confessional, you are a stranger. That's why they have the two separate rooms with just the grill in between."

"I can't believe that Padre Ramon gets many English-speaking women here in this Indian town," I said. "I mean he's either going to think I'm bagging one of the nuns, or sleeping with you, right? That doesn't do my reputation much of good."

"Well listen to you," she mocked. "I didn't know you had a reputation. Lucky me – I'm going with someone who has a reputation to maintain. Are you sure you wouldn't be better off in banking? You could wear a pinstripe suit that distracts the eye from your potbelly."

"Come on, you know what I mean."

"What I say to Padres Ramon has nothing to do with you. It doesn't have anything to do with him, either. It just has to do with me and God."

"So, you're going to phone up God with Ramon on the party line, and you mean to tell me he isn't going to listen in? That's not possible! How could he forget something like that? Here I am, living in this man's house and…" I fumbled for the right word.

"And bagging his papal volunteer," she interjected. God, she was quick.

"I didn't say that."

"You said he'd think you were bagging one of the nuns. Is that what you're doing? *Bagging* me?"

By now we had walked to the fountain in the middle of the square, and she turned to face me so abruptly that I bumped into her. For an agonizing second, she tottered, then fell backward into the dry basin, banging her head against a pitted cement gargoyle, and slumping onto the accumulated dead leaves and trash strewn across the bottom. For a terrible instant, it flashed through my mind that I had killed her.

"Ow!" shouted Simone. "Shit, fuck, piss, that hurts!"

"I'm sorry. I didn't mean to do it," I babbled, making ineffectual efforts to lift her up.

Simone waved away my attempts to get her onto her feet and sat on the trash, rubbing the back of her head. "Golly," she said, "First you try to cut off my access to God, then you tell me I'm just another easy lay, then you knock me into a pile of garbage."

I couldn't tell if she was joking. There was a tremble in her voice that might be anger or might simply be the effort of battling the pain. I hoped she was giving me a hard time.

"You're not just another easy lay," I said. "You're a very special easy lay."

The biggest cockroach in Guatemala crawled into view on Simone's collar. This was a four-incher, waving a pair of antennae so long it looked like mutant.

"Don't move," I said, reaching toward her.

"What's the matter?"

I leaned forward to slap the bug away from her neck, hoping to knock it back into the garbage.

Unfortunately, it landed, minus a couple of legs, on Simone's thigh and began to crawl lopsidedly for cover under her knee.

"Oh, crap, get that thing off me!" she squealed, scrambling upward and slapping wildly at her leg. "Oh, God, it's gross!"

I pulled her out of the fountain and made her stand, trembling, while I inspected her for insects. Apparently, the roach had dropped back into the garbage, for though I brushed her down, there was no sign of him.

"Oh, I feel filthy," said Simone, compulsively rubbing her hands on her blue jeans.

"I saved your life," I said. "Those bastards can be mean when they're cornered."

"Yes, and I will be your cheap lay forever," she said, hugging me. "Use me, degrade me if you will. I will never let you go as long as a roach lives in Guatemala."

"Degrade you? What exactly do you have in mind?"

"Forget it. You can be replaced by a can of Raid."

"Let's never argue again," I said. And then, without thinking, I added, "I love you, you know."

"That's twice you've said that. Say it one more time and it will be true."

"What?"

"If you say something three times, it's yours for life. Like in spelling classes in the sixth grade. Sister Veronica would say, 'Use a word three times and it's yours for life.'"

"And if an Arab says, 'I divorce you,' three times to his wife, she's history," I said.

"Exactly," she said. "So better be careful. You don't want to slip for a third time or you could find yourself committed to some pretty deep shit."

"I'll say it right now," I said.

"Forget it," she said. "You think I want you hanging around all the time?" Then, before I could continue, she said, "Oh look, the store's open. Let's run and get a couple of beers."

I looked over my shoulder to see the same rectangle of light that had beckoned that first night. Inside, two men were seated at a small, plain, wooden table, their heads tilted toward one another in conversation. Alfredo, the short, dark storeowner, was looking directly at us while speaking to a man we had never seen before. As the stranger gesticulated with his cigarette, Alfredo's gaze followed the glowing end in sympathy. Out in the square, I couldn't hear a word, but the conversation exuded conspiracy.

"Maybe we shouldn't go in," I said, holding back. "They look as if they're doing something serious."

"Alfredo?" Simone's tone was incredulous. "Alfredo couldn't harm a fly. And it's my turn to buy."

She started walking toward the store so quickly that I couldn't express my doubts. I scrambled after her and hurried across the dark barren square.

When Simone reached the doorway, Alfredo's eyes darted up and he began to rise, wiping his palms on the towel tucked into his belt. As he pushed back the chair, his gaze returned to the stranger and he lifted his eyebrows almost imperceptibly, as if to say, "The ones we were talking about."

The stranger looked over his shoulder, and I saw the fair skin and hawk nosed profile of a *blanco-blanco*, A slang term for upper class Guatemalan. He wasn't dressed in a uniform, but there was something about him that shrieked "cop". His glance was casual, but contained an element of cool appraisal, as if he were preparing a description for a wanted poster – male, Caucasian, five feet eight with brown hair, brown eyes, no identifying features. As he stood, I realized that he was taller than me by a couple of inches. His hair was combed back carefully in an unstylish pompadour.

"Pleased to meet you," he said in English, reaching for my hand. "I'm Gerardo Villa-Alba. Alfredo was just telling me there was a new *gringo* in the village." He spoke almost without an accent.

"Is that what you do for a living? Count *gringos*?" I could have kicked myself for my excessively hostile and paranoid tone.

"Oh, no," he said. "I'm just a, how do you say it - a salesman for the Formost Corporation. Now that electricity and refrigerators are coming to the countryside, there is a growing market for milk products to improve the diet."

"Too bad you didn't sign up with the Gallo Brewery," said Simone. "You'd make a mint at fiesta time. I don't think that milk is going to be a big seller here in Tecpan."

After a barely imperceptible pause in which Villa-Alba deciphered "big seller," his face lit with forced amusement. "Perhaps we could mix the milk with a shot of rum. That would improve the diet and let the *inditos* celebrate at the same time."

Alfredo had been listening to our conversation in English with apparent consternation, but when he heard *"inditos"*, a nasty term for the native population, his face broke into a smile.

"We're surrounded by a flock of *inditos* here," he said in Spanish. "They're just like parrots. They can talk, but they don't understand a word they say." He followed this comment with a burst of laughter, as if he had made a witticism, but none of us joined in.

"I hate it when the Ladinos talk like that about Indians," Simone said to me in English, as if she were unaware that Villa-Alba could understand every word she said. "You might as well be in Georgia hearing the crackers talk about the 'nigras.'" Then she turned back to Alfredo and said in English. "*Dos cervesas*, please, Alfredo. Do you have any cold ones?"

"Sorry, *senorita*, all I have are warm ones. I only have three bottles left. The Gallo truck comes through tomorrow and you and the other *gringo* are the only ones who drink them cold."

"Shit," said Simone. "Two warm ones, then," she added in Spanish.

"Your English is excellent," I said to Villa-Alba in English to remind Simone that we weren't free to talk as usual. "Have you lived in the United States?"

"No, just a good school in the capital. And I was stationed at Fort Bragg when I was in the army, but that was a long time ago and I was only there for six months."

"What did they teach you in North Carolina?" asked Simone. "Whuppin' slaves as dey picked de cotton?"

Villa-Alba looked confused. "No, no cotton picking. I was just there for a short course. I had to be in the army, you see, because my parents sent me to the military school. They thought it would be a good job for me, but I didn't want to be a soldier. So, I resigned my commission, and now I'm selling milk." He gave a self-deprecating shrug of his shoulders.

"And you," he continued. "What brings you here to Guatemala? You are not tourists." He said this as a statement of fact, as if he were trying to rule out an obvious and unbelievable explanation and save himself the need to destroy it.

"Refugees," said Simone, lifting the warm beer to her lips. "Jim and I are refugees from a power that seeks world domination. Starting from its base in Irkutsk, it has already taken over China and India. Next will come North America and then South America. There's no hope resisting it. Father Ramon, the priest in the mission here is the mastermind. No one knows why a man of the cloth should be so aggressive."

"Man of the cloth?" Villa-Alba looked confused but interested.

"She's talking about Father Ramon's plan to sell Indian textiles in the United States, " I said. "It's a kind of a joke."

"You are very funny," said Villa-Alba , and I hoped he would think he had caught on. "But tell me, what do you really do?" He was looking at me, giving me the impression that he already knew what Simone really did.

"Research on tropical moths," I answered.

"Surely there are no tropical at this altitude. Tecpan is in the cold zone, not the hot."

"Simone invited me to come for a visit. I'm taking a break from my research."

Simone guffawed. "R and R with a little T and A thrown in."

Villa-Alba's eyes snapped back to her as he lost track of her reference. "R and R?" he asked in a pleasantly puzzled tone.

"It's a private code," Simone explained.

"Anyway, I'm going back to Palin tomorrow," I said. "Don't worry, I've collected enough moths to bury an army."

"What army would you like to bury?" asked Villa-Alba. "Not the Guatemalan army, I hope."

"After what I saw on the road coming back from the capital, I wouldn't mind," said Simone.

"On the road?" He was leading her on and I hastened to intervene.

"We saw an arrest," I cut in. "It was a little rough."

"A little rough! It was torture!" Simone was indignant.

"The police are a real problem in this country," said Villa-Alba. Then he added, I thought a bit too obviously, "That's why I left the army. I saw things that were really excessive."

"Look at the time," I said, glancing obviously at my watch. "If I'm leaving early in the morning, we'd better get back to the mission."

"*Gracias, don* Alfredo," said Simone, with exaggerated politeness, handing her empty over the counter. Poor Alfredo accepted it with gratitude. He'd been standing attentively listening to a conversation he couldn't understand.

"See you later, Alfredo," I said in Spanish and waved my half full bottle in a friendly farewell.

I waited until we were across the square before I assailed Simone in whispered tones. "Why did you have to talk like that? Couldn't you see that guy was a government spy?"   "Of course," she said, though I wondered whether she knew or was just covering up her ignorance. "I just wanted to give him something to write in his report. Nothing ever happens in Tecpan. It's too close to the Panamerican Highway. The poor guy must be bored out of his mind."

"Well, you gave him plenty. We're just talking in code - a conspiracy to undermine the free world. When his report gets to Guatemala City, they'll be ready to send out a division."

"People like Villa-Alba are nothing, nothing at all," said Simone.

"They may be nothing to you and me," I said. "But they carry guns and when guns shoot, people find themselves with holes in their guts."

"You're so cute when you try to talk tough," she said. "It just makes me want to tweak your little bottom."

"I'm serious," I said. "We could get in big trouble."

She goosed me and ran away laughing like a junior high school student. I was so startled that I didn't catch her until she'd reached to the mission, and when I snatched her hand away from the knob I was laughing as hysterically as she was. I kissed her, and we caught our breath, and I decided that Simone was right. Villa-Alba was nothing, nothing at all.

*   *   *   *   *   *   *

My departure from the mission the next morning was accomplished with gravity more appropriate to a world tour than a four-hour drive out of the highlands. Maria served up burned eggs in *ranchero* sauce with a stack of black corn tortillas on the side. Padre Ramon, who never stirred from his room before 11:00 unless he had to say Mass, harrumphed up to the table at 7:45. Father Mike worked the importance of driving carefully into the conversation at least three times.

Precisely how they know I was leaving was never clear. I had only decided for certain the night before, during the conversation with the ominous Villa-Alba. There was certainly no pressure for me to leave. No one had even asked what my plans for the week might be. I had arrived and taken up residence. Now I was leaving, and as if by some telepathic power, the family had been called together to witness my departure.

The conversation around the table had the jovial tone reserved for such occasions, with hearty assurances that I should return whenever I wished, and laments about missed opportunities to show me some aspect of local geography. Several pointed references were made to my next visit. I was informed that I simply had to see Tecpan during Holy Week and given graphic accounts of the local celebrations.

All this bonhomie did little to dispel my gloom. The mentions of Holy Week merely made the impending arrival of MacElwain a more prominent feature of my conscious thought. By lingering with Simone, I had guaranteed that there would be an enormous gap in my data on the lunar cycle. In the dim light of morning, I was certain that my thesis could be rejected on these grounds alone. I might even be dropped from the program and forced to confront a draft board ravenous for undeferred bodies.

When Simone said that she would walk me to the truck, the rest politely found other errands and made their excuses. They treated us like a pair of high school students who should be given time for a little innocent petting. The thought of Simone's pending confession danced again in my mind.

What would she say? "I slept with him six times, father." What if her conscience required full disclosure: "And then in the shower I performed oral sex while he…"? "We used condoms until he ran out, and then relied on *coitus interruptus*". For all I knew, the birth control might make Padre Ramon angriest of all. I could return to find the peaceable man armed with a shotgun.

Simone stopped at the doorway. "I'll say goodbye here. I hate long farewells."

"Simone," I began. "About confession."

"I thought about that last night," she said. "I've decided to save up a hundred mortal sins and confess them all at once. It will blow Padre Ramon away!"

Then she pecked me on the cheek, a virginal kiss such as one might give a cousin upon his return from college and walked quickly back into the mission. I turned and went out the door, with nothing more than my backpack to carry with me.

The Scout's gears chattered pleasantly, and the roar of the engine kept me company as I drove along. The vistas along the highway were no less beautiful because they were being seen for the second time, and when I turned off the road into Palin in mid-afternoon, I had the sense, entirely new to me, that I was returning to surroundings familiar and welcoming.

Guillermo was waiting for me in the back room of my house. He might have been there for days. "The police got Riguberto," he said. "They picked him up last Saturday on the Panamerican Highway."

"I know," I answered. "I saw it happen. They were beating him pretty bad."

"How?"

"It was just by chance. I didn't know until they dragged him from the car. There was nothing I could do."

"Riguberto's tough," said Guillermo, with more hope than conviction. "They won't get anything out of him. Where have you been? I thought they might have got you too."

"I was staying with some *gringos* in the highlands." There was no need to tell more and get Simone mixed up in this.

"You were smart not to come back here right away," said Guillermo. "If the police broke Riguberto, they would have come here the first thing."

CHAPTER 7

"Science is what is important," said MacElwain. "As you get older you will discover that truth. These political struggles and petty rivalries will have no impact on the future whatsoever. Science enables us to discover what is true, and once we understand the universe, we gain power over it. All science is one. Each advance in knowledge supports the rest. Sometimes it may seem that understanding the way that temperature controls insect behavior is trivial, but once we have proved that, man will have taken the first step to realizing that the flow of energy through an ecosystem determines its destiny."

He paused his tirade to reach for a second piece of toast from the basket on the table. Wielding his knife like a scalpel, he shaved a curl of butter from the pat on his plate, and spread it across the crumbling surface, smeared a patina of jelly over the butter, and nibbled at the result with yellow, crooked teeth. He lifted the cup of heavily sweetened coffee to his lips and patted away crumbs and coffee drips alike with the corner of his cloth napkin.

Everything about him repelled me. He had missed a spot when shaving that morning, and a tuft of whiskers grew, asymmetrically near the cleft of his chin. He had parted his hair immediately above his left ear, pulling the fringe diagonally forward across a shining expanse of scalp. When he showered, the hair on that side must hang as far as his shoulders. Worst of all, his lips kept working against one another, even when he finished talking. His watery blue eyes stared at me, unflinching and examining. They were the eyes of a high school principal, practiced at unnerving schoolboys brought before him.

I couldn't think of anything to say, so I lifted my hand and motioned for the waitress to bring more coffee. MacElwain sat waiting me out. What was I supposed to say? "Today thermal determinism; tomorrow, the world"?

"Knowledge is power," I muttered unconvincingly.

"Only if we do our work well. You just have to be exhaustive about each datum, and all of the data must be in line. If there are any gaps, the other side will use them to discredit the whole argument. Binsfield's especially unscrupulous."

His voice trailed off. Perhaps he was trying to control himself at the thought of his arch-rival. Binsfield was not only the chair at Stanford; he had once been caught, during an unpredictable moment of silence, snickering to a colleague during one of MacElwain's presentations. Only a few, gasped words were audible to those around him, but the uncontrolled mirth they produced in the colleague was enough to send a sympathetic ripple of laughter across the room. I hadn't been lucky enough to be there, but it was a story told to me a half dozen times.

"I noticed that you missed a night's observations five months ago, and then another in the data you sent at

Christmas," he went on, his tone censorious. "It is absolutely essential that you cover every night."

Oh brother, I thought, what's he going to make of my stay in Tecpan? Six glorious nights of zero data. He'd already frowned with displeasure when I said I'd forgotten to bring my latest notes with me.

"Sometimes it's hard to get out. I've had some bouts with *turista* that were not to be believed."

"Everyone's responsible for his health," MacElwain announced. "Tourists stay at the Camino Real, drink the water, and complain when they get sick. Do they think just because the Hilton is American owned it has its own water system? That's why I always stay here at the Panamerican. Locals understand parasites much better than foreigners. They wash their fruit in purified water. I found that out the first time I came in here in 1954."

As if to prove his trust in the infallibility of the hotel staff, he lifted his water glass with a flourish and washed down the last of his toast.

"Out in the countryside we don't get deliveries of purified water," I said. A night at the Panamerican would have used up a third of my monthly stipend.

His eyes turned, inexplicably, toward the tablecloth. "I won't be able to visit you for a week and a half.," he said. "I've decided to head east to Jutiapa to examine some of the mountainous regions. I've been thinking of a grant proposal to blanket the area with a dozen graduate students, a kind of saturation sampling. I've…" He paused for a moment. "I've reason to believe I could succeed with a grant to cover the expenses."

"National Science Foundation?" I asked. What kind of bullshit was this?   When I left Berkeley, all the talk had been of government cuts in pure research monies. And where was MacElwain going to get twelve graduate students? I was his only advisee in recent memory.

"No, not NSF," he said. "It's actually money that might come through the Department of Agriculture. I understand that they are breaking out of their pattern of only doing applied work in the United States. There are some real opportunities for research support."

"I'm surprised that you're considering sending students to the east of the country," I said. "From what I hear, there's still a great deal of guerilla activity over there."

"Oh, the army cleared that up a year ago. This Arana-Osorio really knows how to handle things. Once he gets elected president, Guatemala is really going to settle down."

"*Time* magazine said he killed 25,000 people chasing 250 communists. They say it's not even certain he got the communists. They may simply have fled back north."

"He got 'em," MacElwain snapped. He caught himself and cleared his throat. "At least, everything that I've read has indicated that the east is totally peaceful."

"So is a cemetery," I said.

It was a standard riposte, and he took it with ease.

"I think it's good to be young and idealistic the way you are. What was it that Churchill said? 'If a young man isn't a liberal, he has no heart. If an old man isn't a conservative, he has no brain.'"

I hated being patronized, but what could I say? I'd been through these conversations before.

"I'd like another coffee," I said, filling the time. MacElwain made an exaggerated look at his wristwatch.

"Look at the time," he said. "I've got an appointment at the embassy at nine." Did he expect me to wait around all morning?

"Where do you want me to meet you?" I asked.

"Oh, well, I'm not sure just how long this will take. It could be quite a while. I'll send you a telegram when I'm done in the east and we can get together in a week or more."

A reprieve, a week without MacElwain! I couldn't believe my luck. Let him make me get up at six to drive to the capital to keep him company at breakfast. I'd do it daily. And he was headed east. Maybe the guerillas would kill him there. They couldn't all be dead.

"All I have on me is a ten-quetzal bill," he said. As if he couldn't put the breakfast on his room bill!

"Don't worry. I'm sure you have to go," I said. "You can buy breakfast another time."

"I'll send you a telegram," he said awkwardly. In fifteen seconds, he had disappeared toward the taxi stand.

I leaned back, lit a Belmont, and waved to the waitress to bring me another coffee.

*   *   *   *   *   *   *   *

*

The telegram lay on my concrete floor where the delivery boy had shoved it under the door. The paper was folded over and crimped back, so that only the address showed.

"Oh, shit," I said aloud. He had decided not to go east. I'd have to drive back and see him tomorrow.

I opened the envelope with dreary apprehension. It was in English.

Situation desperate. World domination no longer satisfied the leader. Yah Zee controls his every waking thought. Will arrive Friday at noon in exile from insufferable regime. Love   Simone

I hope you won't think me melodramatic if I say that I never had despair turn to joy so suddenly. One moment MacElwain's face had intruded in my consciousness, cloaked in nebulous terrors of my academic inadequacy. The next, Simone was in his place, not only in his place but due to arrive in a few minutes. There was no other bus from the capital she could be taking. I had no time to straighten up my house, only a minute to splash some water from the cistern in the patio on my hair, run a comb though the snarls, and set off running for the plaza.

When I turned the corner, I saw that she was already there. She was bending down talking to one of the old Indian women who populated the sidewalks with their baskets of limes, oranges, tortillas, or avocados. As I came pelting down the side street, she straightened up and I could see an avocado in her hand.

"Ho," I said, breathless from my run, though I'd only covered three blocks. "Boy, it's great to see you!" It was hard not to sound like an idiot to myself.

She gave me a hug restrained by the backpack she had in one hand and the avocado she had in the other. "Hold on a second, I'll get you one too."

"She moves in beauty as the night," I said. "Bearing avocados as her delight. That's Keats, isn't it?"

"Byron," she said, and turned to the woman. "How much if I buy two?"

"Two *centavos* more," the old woman replied. "They are two apiece. Two and two are four."

"How about three for the pair?" Simone asked good-naturedly, digging for change.

The old woman shook her head. "No, two *centavos* each."

"He's my *marido*," said Simone, pointing to me. "He'll starve if I don't give him food."

The woman laughed. "Take it then. A woman must make her husband fat."

Simone gave her the extra penny and we walked away together. "I love to bargain with the women," she said. "If you just pay what they ask, it's like you can't stand dealing with them, you'll pay anything to get away from them."

"And I thought you were just cheap," I said.

"That's me, the cheap slut from Altoona, PA," she said. "And who do I have to blame for that, might I ask?" As she was talking, she deftly twisted one of the avocados in half, revealing the green golden flesh. "I always carry a little spoon and a plastic bag with salt," she went on. "'Cause I love avocados so much." The salt was produced from a folded envelope in the left front pocket of her jeans, a battered teaspoon from the right pocket. She spooned out a golden, ripe chunk and savored it. "A minus," she announced. She filled the spoon, sprinkled the contents with salt, and held it out to me.

"So, we're a one spoon couple now," I said. "How intimate."

"Listen to the man," she said. "He spends a week shoving his tongue down my throat every time we kiss, but he's nervous about sharing a spoon."

"Well, I really don't care for avocados," I said. I'd never thought about equating French kissing to using the same silverware.

"I've got to tell you everything that's happening at the mission," she began in a breathless tone. "That cop we met in Alfredo's store is back in town, staying in the *palacio municipal,* and a squad of army men has moved in as well. They're looking for guerillas by driving up and down the back roads at night. As if the guerillas wouldn't hear them coming the way they gun the motors at seven at night."

"Pretty obvious, huh?"

"Oh, and I played the most wonderful trick on them!" She giggled like a three-year-old. "One afternoon a group was returning on foot from the mountains west of town, so I ran to the municipal police screaming that a group of guerillas were heading for town. The mayor jumped on the phone and called someone, and a couple hours later a helicopter is overhead. By this time, it was getting dark, so they dropped a flare and set fire to the shed outside town where Maria keeps her cows! By this time the patrol had arrived and they started shooting into the shed. It was so funny."

"You're lucky you didn't get caught in the crossfire," I said. "And what about Maria's cows?"

"You're as bad as Padre Ramon. The cows hadn't been driven in yet, and Maria's all over the government for the loss of her shed. I wanted to suggest that she threaten to make them eat her soup until she was compensated, but Father Mike said I should be polite."

We'd turned the corner onto my street and the front door loomed ahead. "I hope you don't expect something as nice as the mission. Actually, it's a dump."

"So it is," she said, once inside the door. "And I thought I was going to check into a Holiday Inn."

"Here's the second room," I said, like a real estate salesman showing the property.

"A well-equipped house," said Simone. "I see you have a year's copies of *Playboy* in the corner. They look as if they're been read a good deal."

"Actually, I just look at the pictures," I said. "I wouldn't be caught dead reading the fiction. I understand they actually have a story by Norman Mailer in one of them."

"Shocking," she said. "The way some people try to pass off culture as smut."

"How do you know about *Playboy*? I didn't know good Catholic girls were allowed such stuff. Didn't you have to take a pledge not to read it?"

"I didn't buy them. Tommy kept them stuffed under his mattress."

"Tommy?"

"A guy I went with in high school."

"Well, I'm going to throw my hoard away for you. Your body is far more beautiful than any centerfold. I bet Tommy wouldn't do that for you."

"No, it was Tommy's mother who threw his *Playboys* away when she found them. It was nice that he had one vice she didn't blame on me."

"So, he wouldn't have dumped them in comparison with your beautiful body?"   "Tommy was the one with the beautiful body. He was a swimmer in high school and he looked fantastic. He had wide shoulders, narrow hips, rippling muscles – the works. I could never compete with that."

"So, you were after him for his body, the way you are with me?"

She laughed. "I used to shave him before his swim meets. His mother was working, so we had the house to ourselves. We'd get in the shower together with a can of Barbasol and a Gillette."

"Young and in love, kismet with shaving cream all over it. And was Tommy as sweet as I am?"

"Oh, none of that," she answered, her voice matter of fact. "We were just a couple of kids enslaved by our hormones."

CHAPTER 8

She was lying, of course. Tommy was sweet,
and she'd known it ever since the day after her family
moved into the house on Adler Street. She looked out
the bedroom window and saw him walking off to
Vacation Bible School at the First Presbyterian Church
of Altoona. His hair was slicked down and the part was
as straight as if it had been laid out with a ruler. She
could see the white of his socks between the cuffs of his
blue jeans and the tops of his sneakers, and he didn't roll
up the sleeves on his T shirt the way the boys who went
to Saint Anthony's did. Still, he didn't look fruity, and
he was big enough and strong enough that bullies
wouldn't pick on him. She guessed he was a year ahead
of her in school, which meant he'd be entering junior
high in the fall.

"What are you looking at?" her sister, Veronica,
asked from the twin bed on the far side of the room.

"Oh, just some boy next door," said Simone, a
little too carelessly.

"Hey, Patrick," Veronica yelled without even
getting up to look out. "Simone's in love with the boy
next door."

"I am not," said Simone.

Patrick's leering face appeared in the doorway.
"Watch' a lookin' for, Simone? Hope his barn door's
open and his horse will come out?"

"Pimple butt."

"I bet you'd love to see it."

Patrick had been impossible ever since, Bobby, the oldest brother, turned sixteen and started driving. The two would take the Plymouth and cruise Route 30, smoking cigarettes and chewing cinnamon Life Savers to cover the smell on their breath. She hated them. They thought they were so hot.

"I'll tell Mom about the copy of *Playboy* you have under your mattress."

Patrick lunged across the groom, grabbed her and punched her arm so hard she almost started to cry. "I'll kill you, you little shit!" he snapped.

She cowered back against the headboard of her bed, tears stinging the inside of her eyelids. "I hate you!" she said.

She knew she wouldn't tell. She couldn't be so evil, no matter how much she hated Patrick. To tell was the worst thing you could do. That night her mother noticed the bruise when she was kissing Simone good night and said, "Now where did that come from?" in an absent-minded way.

"I bumped against the banister when I tripped on the stairs this morning," said Simone, pulling the sleeve of her nightgown down over the blue mark.

"Maybe your father should check the banister to make sure it isn't loose," her mother said as a kind of reflex. She would never mention it. Bruises were an incidental part of her great task of stretching an electrician's income to feed and clothe six children, meet mortgage payments, and still cover the costs of parochial school tuition.

"Honestly, Catherine," other women said. "I don't know how you do it." Her mother's satisfaction radiated then. She didn't have to mention the shopping at the JC Penney Annual Spring Sale, the stitching of unmatched socks onto pajama pants legs to extend their life for an extra three months, the folding of paper towels to serve as napkins at family meals. The women of her parish shared their routines, and the daily rituals of frugality set the rhythm of their lives. At least Tom had enough seniority in the local he didn't have to worry about layoffs.

That Saturday, Simone carried the lie into the confessional as one of the small hoard of childish sins she accumulated for Father Bartholomew. "I fibbed to my mother four times," she said, counting the time she wore her underwear a second day even though her mother hadn't actually asked if it was clean.

"And do you repent of these sins?" asked Father Bartholomew. There was a line outside the confessional with at least two teenaged girls with far more substantial matters to whisper through the grill.

"Yes, Father," said Simone, and went to say her Hail Mary's and Our Fathers, cleansing her soul to receive the host.

Simone talked to Tommy for the first time when Mrs. Bergman brought over an apple pie two days later to repay the casserole Simone's mother had cooked a week earlier as a welcome to the neighborhood. "To look us over", said Simone's mother. "I saw her staring at the crucifix on the wall. She's a cool one."

Simone was surprised by the bitterness in her mother's voice, for Catherine seldom permitted the children to see her being critical of anyone. She and Mrs. Bergman would circle one another with offensive correctness for the remainder of their lives. Neither was willing to give the other legitimate cause for complaint. Cards were exchanged at Christmas. Pleasant nods and standard greetings were never omitted when passing on the street or in chance encounters at the Krogers.

Tommy and Simone were sent to the rumpus room in the basement while their mothers built their fortifications over coffee. They played Sorry! without enthusiasm and munched on the bowl of potato chips with which Catherine had matched the apple pie.

"I hate it when parents make you go somewhere and play, don't you?" asked Simone.

"Yeah, it's really stupid," said Tommy.

"Every time my mother says, 'She has a daughter just your age so you'll have a wonderful time,' it makes me want to spit."

"Yeah," said Tommy, picking up the dice cup. "It's stupid. Do you know why the little moron cut the toilet seat in half?"

"No, why?"

"Because he heard his half-assed cousin was coming to visit."

Simone didn't really understand this, since her father was scrupulously correct in his language at home, but she laughed anyway, because she knew she was supposed to.

"I bet you children are getting along wonderfully," called Mrs. Bergman from the top of the stairs. She was coming down to fetch Tommy.

"Yeah," said Tommy, without enthusiasm.

"Say it's been nice meeting you," prompted his mother.

"It's been nice meeting you," he mumbled.

The two of them would not speak again until Simone was in the tenth grade. There was never anything as dramatic as a prohibition, but the walls of separation in Altoona were impregnable. Boys didn't play with girls, for one thing, and Tommy's mother compelled her son to live a life of diligence and achievement. His afternoons were filled with baseball practice in the summer and swimming at the YMCA during the school year. There could be no leisure until all his homework was complete and his mother had verified it. Virtually the only time Simone saw him was when he cut the grass, marching from one hedge to another.

She did not pine for him or long to speak with him again. He was relegated to an inconsequential part of her environment, like the maple tree in the front yard or the Dobson twins the women cooed over each Sunday after mass.

During these years, Simone's Catholic virginity was the focus of a concerted campaign of preservation. Confirmation classes were long past, but the parish sponsored heavily chaperoned CYO outings, roller skating parties, and church dances designed to provide its youth with appropriately Catholic friends of the opposite sex. The length of a kiss, the place's a boy's hands could touch, and the subsequent feelings were subjected to searching analysis.

"Why don't you just say, 'If it feels good, it's out?' Simone asked Sister Mary Elizabeth and spent two weeks doing penance under the supervision of the assistant principal.

It was Mrs. Bergman's ambition for Tommy that proved her undoing. When he entered the tenth grade, the Bergmans sat down to plan Tommy's college finances, and rose with a decision -- Mrs. Bergman would try to get full-time hours at the Thrifty Drugstore. By freezing casseroles on the weekend and setting the oven timer, she could arrive home at five and still have dinner on the table by a quarter of six.

"Tommy's not even here most afternoons. It's either baseball practice or swimming practice, so there's hardly any mess around the house."

Three weeks later, and a blustery day in early March, Simone was carrying the trash out after school and saw Tommy on his back porch smoking a cigarette. "I didn't know you smoked," she said, emptying the basket into the garbage can.

"Want one?" he asked, holding out the pack with two filter tips protruding above the foil.

"We should go inside," she said, scrambling through a gap in the hedge. "My mom will kill me if she sees me."

"My mom will kill me if she smells smoke in the house," said Tommy, so they crawled under the wooden steps, screened from view by the crosshatched side grating. Squeezed together, they were suddenly aware of how close their bodies were and Tommy laughed nervously as he held out the match.

"And then he kissed you," I said.

"No, then we smoked a cigarette," she said. "It was my first Winston. I said, 'Won't this ruin your wind for swimming?' He said, 'Swimming's stupid. I hate it.' I asked him why he did it, and he said his mother made him. She thought he could get a scholarship to a good school, but no school was going to give a scholarship to the champion of Juniata County, with the thirty-seventh best time in the state. I said I knew how he felt."

"And then he kissed you," I said.

"No, then it started to rain and I went home and took the garbage back into the kitchen, if you must know."

"So, the shaving cream came later," I said.

I'd been worming the story out of her all afternoon, bringing the topic up over the plate of eggs and beans served for lunch at Dona Felicia's kitchen, returning to questions about Altoona as we walked out into the fields, even though I could see talking about it depressed her. I was obsessed with the image of the two of them in the shower, appalled Tommy had a body more attractive than mine. It was the play, the innocence of what she described, the sudden intensity of pleasures honed by a billion years of evolution to drive the species onward. Tommy became my rival, the man in her life whose place I could never take, because he was the first and I would be one of many. I pushed and wheedled even though I could see she was becoming more withdrawn as we talked.

"What did your mothers think of this?" I asked.

"We managed to keep our friendship a secret for about two weeks, but when he asked me out to the Spring Fling at the public high school, there was no avoiding it. What could they say? I mean, since

Kennedy had got elected you could hardly say anything against it. My mother just looked worried, and my sister told me to wear a panty girdle. Tommy said his mother just said, 'Now I understand why I'm getting notes from Coach Mueller." She was sure I had lured him away from practice. But really there was nothing they could do once we just went ahead and said we were going out."

"The Spring Fling," I chortled, trying to break the tension. "It must have been a trip."

"The usual thing," she said. "Paper streamers from basket to basket in the high school gym, and a DJ at one end playing requests. We had a good time, sort of. I didn't know any of the girls there and that was all right by me. Tommy punched out a kid who asked him if he was getting any, but it happened in the boys room so I only heard about it later. Then we went out and parked but he got me home five minutes early. The lights were on in the living room, but he kissed me on the front porch anyway. I think it was a big thing for him."

"Quite a lurid affair for you too."

"Oh, no. The Catholic boys were all Mister Happy Hands compared to Tommy. One time, Jimmy LaVeccio reached inside my bra when he had a long sleeved shirt on and got his cuff button caught. Sister Angelica was coming down the hall and he was swearing and trying to get it loose. It was really funny."

"He was feeling you up in school?"

"It was a two-school dance between Our Lady's and Juniata Catholic. After Saint Anthony's there were either boys schools or girls schools. The boys all wore blue blazers and striped ties. The nuns and priests patrolled the dance, but as long as there were lookouts, nobody got caught."

"So, Jimmy LaVeccio was your first love?" Here was a chance to dethrone Tommy once and for all.

"No, Jimmy was just my way of putting down Carol Ann Barnes for bragging about how she French kissed Alan Yates."

"You give me an entirely new vision of adolescent girls," I said. "My friends and I thought we were so tough."

"Jimmy was tough enough. He ended up in Morganza, a reform school, for stealing cars. He was really just joy riding, but the judge was up for reelection and wanted to make an example of him. He sure couldn't kiss. Even in ninth grade I knew that."

"Could Tommy kiss?" Why did I have to keep on asking?

"I'm bored with this conversation and I'm not going to talk anymore. I'm going to sleep."

We were lying on the mattress by that time, and when I reached for her, she turned away and curled up, hugging her knees to her chest. I stroked her shoulder tentatively, but she didn't say anything. From the way she was lying on the bed, she might have been sucking her thumb. I ran my hand down her arm, but she didn't move.

I flopped back and stared up at the ceiling. Maybe she would leave tomorrow. Maybe I would never sleep with her again, never even see her again. I guessed that she wouldn't make a scene. She would just throw her things in her backpack, walk down to the square, and take a bus out of my life.

"Simone," I ventured. "I'm sorry."

"That's OK," she said. "It will be all right in the morning. Let's get some sleep."

I wanted to touch her again, but instead I lay there with my arms at my sides, like a corpse on a slab, until her regular breathing told me she was asleep. Then I lifted myself from the mattress, inched back into my Levis, and felt my way into the dark of the front room. My jacket was over the back of the chair, with cigarettes and matches in the pocket. I slipped the bolt and stood in the doorway, looking into the street as I smoked.

The waning moon was in its final quarter, still bright enough to wash the town in light. Everything was still. The next time the moon was full I would gather data conclusively disproving thermal determinism. I wondered how I would explain the missing days of my visit to Tecpan to MacElwain. The gap would give him the opportunity to claim my research was flawed and reject my dissertation. Anyone who glanced at the results could see the moths were keyed to the lunar cycle. Changes in temperature had nothing to do with their behavior. I couldn't hide the data much longer.

I dropped the cigarette butt into the road and kicked a little pile of dust over it with my bare toes. God, I hated MacElwain. What was I doing in Guatemala chasing moths? Tomorrow Simone would leave, then MacElwain would arrive back from the eastern departments of Guatemala, and in six months I'd be in Berkeley with no deferment.

The smoke from the cigarette filtered up through the dirt like wisps of steam from a once dormant volcano. I turned back, slid the bolt on the door, and crept onto the mattress.

CHAPTER 9

I woke the next morning with a start. Simone was sitting cross-legged on the mattress beside me, her eyes fixed on my chest.

"How long have you been looking at me?"

"About five minutes. I wanted to see if I could rouse you by mental telepathy."

"Well, something woke me up," I said, propping myself on one elbow. She pushed me down again.

"Oh no," she said. "You have become Madame Simone's Love Slave. I stole your spirit last night and you must lie completely still until I reintegrate it with your body."

"How do you propose to do that?"

"It may take quite a while and involve considerable friction," she said. "You must not rise until Madame Simone gives you permission." She began lightly stroking my chest. "Let me see now," she said, as her fingers caressed my nipples, "Madame Simone must find the spiritual center of her Love Slave's being."

"That tickles!"

"Down, Love Slave."

"But…"

"Love Slave must not rise," she said, pressing against my chest.

"Well, part of me is starting to rise, whether Madame Simone orders it or not."   "Ah, we are approaching the center!" She lifted her hands from my chest and drew her night gown up over her head, tossing it against the wall on the far side of the room.

"This could be fun," I said with a nervous laugh. I wasn't completely comfortable with being on the bottom.

"Lie still, Love Slave. These rituals must be done in just the right way."

"Could Madame Simone remove her Love Slave's jockey shorts? Love Slave's privates are nearly bent double."

"Madame Simone sees all," she said. "By the time Madame Simone is finished with her Love Slave, limp will be the magic member and bending will not be a problem."

As so, of course, her prediction came true. We joined our bodies with the gleeful abandon of a Halloween prank, as if pleasure was all that mattered in the universe. In the end, I was permitted at last to raise myself on my elbow and look at her body sprawled across the tumbled sleeping bags.

"Simone," I said, "I never met anyone like you."

"That's right," she said, her voice shimmering with contentment. "I'm unique. But then, everyone is unique in the sight of God."

"Oh no, God again? I wish you'd keep God out of the room. It's like having a peeping Tom looking over my shoulder every time we screw. It makes me want to jerk on my pants and rush from the room, zipping as I go. That can be very dangerous, you know."

"He could hardly be looking off your shoulder. You were flat on your back."

"You know what I mean. I mean God has nothing to do with us. And anyway, there isn't any God. It's just a fairy tale made up by priests to keep people under their control. I mean, if you really believed in God, how could you make me your Love Slave?"

"'The body is the temple of the soul.' And how could you house a soul inside a temple that's hot to trot? Madame Simone was just giving her humble Love Slave a chance to take his mind off his peter for a change."

"My mind is never off my peter. It's all I live for."

"But James," she said in mock horror. "What about your moths?"

"An assignment."

"What about the war in Vietnam? Surely you must feel something about that?"

"Only relief that I'm not there. As far as I'm concerned, any dumb putz stupid enough to get drafted deserves everything he gets."

"What if they go to Saigon and get laid? Do they deserve that?"

"No, but they probably deserve the VD they get doing it."

"What about the Indians here in Guatemala? That man we saw being tortured on the road? You've got to care about them."

"Guatemala's different. The Indians didn't ask the Spanish to come over here. I mean, Cortez and Alvarado just came in and took over. Someone who goes to Vietnam just because his draft board tells him to has a choice. He could go to Canada."

She looked away. "Maybe they have fewer choices than you think." Her voice was distant, as if she was speaking over the phone from another country.

"But they must know that they're killing people. They can't have been that brainwashed."

"Maybe they think there are worse things than killing people. Maybe it's better to kill someone you don't know than to kill someone you do."

"Anyway," I said, "It's time for breakfast. It won't do anyone any good for us to mortify our bodies with hunger."

"You better watch out, kid," she said. "You've been hanging around those priests too much. You're starting to sound like one of them."

We pulled on our clothes and ambled lazily off to the woman who provided my breakfast of black beans and eggs. It never occurred to me to ask how long she would stay or for her to tell me. There was no strangeness, no getting to know one another. As long as the sex was good, there were no questions to ask. As we sat over breakfast and chatted through mouths stuffed with tortillas, everything that Simone said seemed strange and wonderful. I felt wonderful too, powerful and attractive. For all I knew, we were setting up housekeeping for life. What the hell, it was OK with me if she never left.

It was all so routine I didn't give any thought to the matter of setting out at dusk to do my collecting. At first, I thought Simone would be coming too, but the forests meant snakes and she wasn't about to go tramping about when she couldn't see them. I decided to cut my evening short and told her I would be back by one in the morning. She kissed me goodbye at the door.

"I won't open for anyone until you get back," she said. "Unless it's an old woman selling half poisoned apples. I always deal with them. I like the way the cartoon birds give them a hard time."

"Hi ho. Hi ho. It's off to work I go," I said.

"I wonder which dwarf you are," she said. "Grumpy? Sneezy?" "Sexy, I hope. Or maybe Fucky?"

"Goodbye, Horny," she said, and pushed me away.

Looking back, it is hard not to invest that moment with poignancy. She was the mommy; I was the daddy. She might have been Donna Reed handing her children their lunch bags and pecking her doctor husband on the cheek as they headed off into the outside world. I jumped into the Scout, gunned the motor, and rattled off down the street with a little more dash than normal.

I did a half-hearted job of collecting and was back by 12:15, but I was too late. Guillermo had already been there for three hours. I knew that someone was inside as soon as I turned the corner. The door was open. And the light from my lantern threw a skewed trapezoid of brightness onto the road. It could only be Guillermo at that hour, and he surely would have come before ten. I rolled the Scout to a stop and walked into the house with a firm and even tread. Any suggestion that someone was sneaking up and Guillermo would pull his pistol. I wasn't eager to deal with the kind of questions that would bring up.

"Ola!" I called out in a jovial and welcoming tone, even before I stepped into the light. "It is the wayward traveler returning home!" How could he mistake that?

"Jim," said Guillermo as I stepped into the room. "I've just been having a fascinating conversation with Simone."

"Hi," I said to Simone, who was leaning against the wall taking a long slow drag from a joint. She looked really wasted.

"Having a good time, I see," I said, examining Guillermo closely. His eyes were clear and though he tried to look casual, he must have been faking his tokes.

"Fascinating friends you have, Jim," said Simone. "They certainly know what to bring on a neighborly visit. Beats apple pie all to hell, I can tell you that." She began a giggling fit that might last until morning.

I hoped Guillermo would see how angry I was. He must have known from the gossip around town that someone was staying with me and waited until I was gone before he came over.

"Just how fascinating was the conversation," I asked, staring directly at Guillermo.

"Guillermo is going to let me join the revolution!" said Simone. "I mean I won't kill anybody, but I can help."

"Simone told me all about the fantastic battle of Tecpan," said Guillermo. "A heroic defense of the nation by the troops of our elite military. We had a good laugh about that."

"Guillermo seems to have been talking a great deal. Good old Gabby Guillermo."

"Gabby, Grumpy, Sneezy, and Fucky!" said Simone. "Let's see, what other dwarves were there?"

"When I realized that Simone was simpatico to our cause," said Guillermo, "it was only natural to share our mutual interests."

"What you are doing is great," said Simone. "Fighting for the Indians against the Ladinos. It's about time somebody did something about the way Indians are treated in this country."

"Did Guillermo tell you about the time he tried to blow up a bridge and ended up getting three of his men killed?

"It was an honest mistake," said Guillermo.

"It was incompetence. If this were my country, I'd have him shot."

"It's not your country and it's not your movement," he snapped back. I glanced toward Simone to see how she would respond, but suddenly she was asleep. Sprawled in the corner, she might have been a corpse.

"You bastard," I hissed. "What did you have to go and tell her all this for? She's just a kid. This is nothing for her to get mixed up in."

"Who are you to make those decisions?" He leaned back against the wall and crossed his ankles, as calm in my house as if he owned it. "You drive me through a roadblock and deliver a couple of messages to the capital and you want to take over. You're sympathetic, you're a friend, but you're not my gringo boss."

"For God's sake," I said. "She's a girl. What can she do to help you? If you want a message delivered, I'll deliver it for you."

"She's better than you are, Jim. She doesn't know anything. No one would suspect her. If she does get caught, they'll just throw her out of the country. They don't want to get the church on their backs."

"*Como se dice* asshole *en español*?"

He laughed as if I'd made a joke and heaved himself to his feet.

"I'm going to tell her not to do it," I said.

He gave a broad, knowing smile. "I don't think the young *señorita* is one to be told anything. Don't worry. It's just this once. She'll be in no more danger than if she rode to Tecpan with you as her driver." He seemed to think this last statement was very funny, and he was still chuckling as he turned to corner at the end of the block.

CHAPTER 10

The next morning with Simone was more maddening than my conversation with Guillermo. She alternated between treating her mission as a prank I was absurd to take seriously and talking about it as a blow in the war to save the wretched of the earth. The more I pointed out the dangers, the more excited she became. Any attempt to impugn Guillermo's motives was met with star-struck hero worship.

"Look, Simone," I said. "This isn't a joke. You're not back in high school with Freddy What's-his-name's hand in your bra. If you get caught, you'll be in real danger."

"Are you kidding?" she asked. "You don't know what fear is until you go one on one with a parochial school nun. Sister Catherine could have played right tackle for Notre Dame. I'll never forget the time I got caught writing, 'Sister Kate shit on the gate" on the blackboard. Talk about rough stuff. We had a lay teacher named Mrs. Leggert who wore her braid in a circle on top of her head. We used to chant, 'Old Lady Leggert with a bird's nest on top. Along came a robin and plop, plop, plop!' Well one day, we were chanting and…"

"Damn it, Simone," I shouted. "This isn't a game. You saw what happened to the man on the road. Villa-Alba's already suspicious of you. He could have you deported, killed."

"Villa-Alba is in Tecpan. All I'm doing is carrying some leaflets to the capital. Have you read the stuff they're putting out? Pretty purple prose. The only danger to the Guatemalan army is if they read it and die laughing. Maybe I should donate my literary genius to the cause."

"What would you say? Drop your bombs like this, plop, plop, plop, the way we hit Mrs. Leggert with the water balloons?"

"How did you know about the water balloons?"

"Every American school child has thrown water balloons at a Mrs. Leggert."

"What a great idea for drought-stricken regions. Just invite Elvira Leggert to come to town. Immediately, out of nowhere, hundreds of thousands of school children appear, pelting her with water balloons. The water would run into the fields and the crops be saved. I could get a Nobel Prize for this."

"Simone, you can be as silly as you like, but I'm not going to let you put yourself in danger. You think because you're a girl and a papal volunteer, they won't go after you. They will and they're not going to let a little thing like the Roman Catholic Church stop them."

"That's why I've got to go. If they're as unscrupulous as you say, well then, it's up to everyone to stop them. Otherwise they'll just run things forever and go on treating the Indians like dirt."

"And you're going to stop them by carrying pamphlets to Guatemala City."

"It's better than sitting around doing nothing. The journey of a thousand miles begins with but a single pamphlet. It's in the Bible somewhere. Or was that 'Gather ye pamphlets while ye may?'"

"No, it's gather ye moth wings while ye may. Stay here with me. Come into the jungle and I will show you a place where the water falls into a crystal pool surrounded by trees encrusted with orchids. I will slather your naked body with whipped cream and feast upon you while tropical birds sing."

"And tropical mosquitoes feast on my naked butt," she said. "Thanks, James, I know you're worried about me, but I'll be fine. I have to go back to Tecpan anyway. I'll take the bus to Guatemala City, drop off the stuff at the address, then catch another bus to the highlands. It's no big deal."

"You don't know what you're getting into, Simone."

"And you do? If you'd known what you were getting into, you'd never have let me pick you up at the El Vaquero. Don't worry. I love you and I'll never do anything to hurt you."

"That's once," I said, "Tell me you love me two times more and I'm yours for life."

Maybe it will be all right, I told myself, as I walked her down to the plaza to wait for the bus. It's a girlish prank and if they catch her, they'll probably just send her out of the country. I'll be done with my research in another six months and then I can go to Pennsylvania and see her. Maybe she could enroll at Berkeley and live with me while I write my dissertation.

"What are you thinking about?" asked Simone, as we sat in the plaza, waving away gnats and wondering why the bus was late coming up the road from Escuintla.

"Just planning our wedding," I said. "I see you in a gown of magenta with orange blossoms in your hair. I mean, you could hardly wear white. Maybe I should wear a white tuxedo. You make me feel positively virginal sometimes."

She grabbed my arm in a conspiratorial way and leaned up and kissed my ear. The man selling cigarettes on the corner was watching us, but he didn't move a muscle as he sat beside his makeshift stand.

"When my sister got married last year," Simone giggled, "my mother gave her a book called *Family Life* which she bought in the Catholic Bookstore. Anyway, Mary Louise was talking to Loretta --she's the oldest - and she says, 'Well, I read the book and it all seems to boil down to penetration and ejaculation.' I thought, 'Honey, there's a lot more to it than that.'"

"Simone," I said. "Don't go. Stay with me. I couldn't stand it if something happened to you."

"I've got to get back to Tecpan."

"I don't care about Tecpan. Just don't go getting involved with Guillermo. I really mean it. This stuff is real and it's going to get worse, much worse. We could go back to Berkeley and..."

"Shit," she said, "You weren't kidding about planning a wedding, were you?"

"The magenta dress? No, I was just being silly."

"But you were thinking about being serious about one another. Just my luck. Why do I always get involved with men who start getting serious? Why can't we just have fun?"

"Well, it's what I want too, but it won't be any fun if you go and get yourself killed."

"Tommy was like that. Every time I shaved him, he'd start talking about getting married."

"Fuck Tommy. Tommy has nothing to do with us."

"I don't see why I can't make my own decisions without some idiot boyfriend deciding to take care of me. You think because you've seen me naked, you know everything about me. Did it ever occur to you I might be bad news, and you should save yourself while you can? Oh no, one or two quick rolls in the hay and you're ready to tie yourself to me for life."

The bus rattled into the plaza and swung to a halt at the far corner. The assistant leaped to the pavement before it had even stopped, its worn brakes shrilling. He raced to the back and clambered up the ladder leading to the roof rack.

"Guatemala! Guate! Guate!" he shouted into the empty square. A heavy woman wearing the long, flounced shirts of rural *Ladina* women, climbed out of the front and looked up as he untied a great net of avocados. A porter shuffled over and she shoved a coin in his hand, then headed for the market, not even looking to see if he followed.

"I think in my next life I'll be an assistant on a Guatemalan bus," Simone said. "Hanging over the edge so I can look down the young girls' blouses as they get off, screaming the destination at the top of my lungs to everyone in sight, a different girl in each town. They are the last free men alive."

We were walking across the square toward the waiting bus. "Give me the stuff you have to deliver, Simone. I'll drive you to the capital, put you on a bus to

Tecpan, drop off the pamphlets and come back. Guillermo will have his revolution and I'll have done it. I was a Boy Scout. I can count it as my good deed for the day."

"Patrick was an Explorer Scout until he was fifteen," she said. "Then Father Edward caught the whole post doing a circle jerk on an overnight at Clear Creek campground. I told Patrick it was no news to me. I'd always known he was a jerk-off. Mother was lighting candles at the church for a month over that one."

"Simone, shut up, come back with me, and we'll ride back to the city together. I have a bad feeling about your doing this alone."

"Forget it, Buster," she said. "The next thing you'd have me imprisoned in a split-level house with a mansard roof, two babies, and a bun in the oven. You'll go off every morning to teach at a state teacher's college and blame me for ruining your career. You think I don't know what happens to girls who accept favors from men, but I do."

"Simone," I was pleading now, trying desperately to interrupt the flow of her enthusiasm.

"Well, you're not going to take it away from me."

"Take what away from you?"

"My chance," she said, though who could know what she meant. She jumped up the narrow steps of the bus and lurched back the aisle as the driver ground the gears and moved off. The assistant came running past me, skipped to get his inside foot forward, and jumped onto the first step as the driver ground the gears into second. I was left in a diesel haze as the bus rolled up the narrow street toward the highway.

It will be all right, I said to myself. The police are idiots. If they can't even pick up Guillermo, how could they ever catch Simone? She'll go to some pharmacy in Zone 2 and hand over a package to the clerk. They will exchange double-entendres and code words with a solemnity that would immediately make their behavior stand out as subversive to the most casual observer, but no one will be looking. She'll go back to Tecpan and tell Padre Ramon. She won't be able to keep from bragging about it and there will be nothing else to talk about at the table. He'll get angry and threaten to send her back to the States. She'll give him some backchat, but in the end, she'll settle down. Villa-Alba will leave Tecpan. Even he will be able to see there are no guerillas there. Everything will be all right.

I kept thinking everything would be all right the entire day. I thought it as I put my notes in order and swept out the front room, said it as I spread the sleeping bag in the sun to air it out, and cleaned nests of empty Tot-Trix bags from the corners of the bedroom. After I had collected the Gallo beer bottles and returned them, I sat in the doorway and smoked Belmonts, wishing Simone would have decided to send a telegram boasting of her safe arrival, and hoping it would miraculously arrive in Palin the same day and I would see the delivery boy come around the corner to bring me the news.

No news came that day or the next, and when I found out everything had gone right, it was not a telegram boy that carried the information. It was Villa-Alba.

CHAPTER 11

Villa-Alba's knock, when it came two days later, was soft, but I knew from the second I heard it that this visit would be trouble. Maybe memory is failing me after all this time. Maybe the knowledge of what was to come has caused me to invest the sound with a sinister resonance. We remember events because we know what they mean. Recalling the past is like reading an Agatha Christie for the second time. All the clues point straight to the villain, and when the police see the revolver on the table, we know it was carried in from the garden to frame the young woman. Still, I swear I walked to the door with a sense of dread and paused to wipe my sweating palms on my pants leg before I turned the knob.

He was in uniform, but he wore it with such ease he might have strolled over for a chat after work. He wasn't wearing a hat. The afternoon sun glistened off his fair hair and gave a good-natured flush to his forehead. There was nothing starched about him, and he stood with his weight shifted slightly onto one leg. He smiled. "Do you mind if I come in?" he asked.

"There's only one chair inside," I said. "Maybe we should walk to the central square and sit on a bench. Or I could buy you cup of coffee at a stall in the market."

He shrugged.

"Hold on a second. I'll get my shoes."

I hustled back to the middle room, poking around the sleeping bag in desperation, calling out that I would be there in a minute. My left sneaker was lost in the folds. Finally, I lifted the whole sleeping bag and shook it and the shoe came tumbling out. I jerked it on my foot without bothering to retie it.

Villa-Alba had stepped through the doorway and was fingering the notes on the table in the front room. He picked up a vial with some leaves in it and examined it closely.

"These good to smoke?" he asked, as if he were joking.

"They're samples," I said. "Whenever I collect a specimen, I record the nearest flora. If I don't know the name of a particular plant, I bring back leaves for identification later."

"That's funny," he said. "I thought it was the caterpillar which ate the leaves and not the moth." He looked as if he had scored a point in a debate, catching me out in an obvious lie.

"It's because of the caterpillars the moths must be careful where they breed. I mean, if you only eat the leaves of the ceiba tree, it's no good laying your eggs on a coffee plant."

"These aren't ceiba leaves," he said in a smug tone. "Those are much broader."

"I didn't say these were ceiba leaves," I said. "I was just making up an example." I could feel my neck tightening. I had the devastating sense the man was getting the best of me. I told myself not to lose my temper.

"Let's go for coffee," I added brightly. "I'm dying for a cup and Doña Mariana's stall has the best. Believe me, I know them all."

I moved toward the door, but he stayed perfectly still, holding the glass vial and looking at it. I couldn't get out without pushing past him. I had a nearly uncontrollable desire to shoulder him aside and make a run for it. At the same time, part of me was desperate to keep him out of the back room, the room where Simone and I had made love, as if I were protecting some inner sanctum from desecration.

After a long pause, I launched into an explanation of thermal determinism, my words sounding lame enough to my own ears and surely insincere to him. As I went on about the importance of understanding the environment and the danger of moths to certain crops, my whole life began to seem absurd and implausible. I felt as if I were justifying my existence to an inquisitor. With each detail, I shrank and became laughable. Villa-Alba didn't say a word.

"So, you can see this kind of knowledge is very important economically as well as scientifically," I concluded without conviction.

"You must spend a great deal of time walking around in the forests on the skirts of the volcano," he said.

"Flanks," I said.

"What?"

"In English, the volcano doesn't have skirts, it has flanks or foothills."

He ignored my correction. "Do you ever notice groups of people when you are there? Evidence that a band or patrol might have been moving through the area?"

"Well, there are Indians going to their corn fields every day."

"Do you talk to these farmers?"

"Of course. I've been told it would be impolite to pass without greeting them."

"But you don't talk to them extensively about what they've seen?"

"They're a pretty close-lipped bunch. We just wish each other good journey and go on."

"You haven't seen evidence of groups moving around in the forest itself?"

"Do you mean like a guerilla band camping out? No, nothing like that. Maybe we should go for coffee now." I was beginning to hope he might just have come to pump me for details because I spent a great deal of time in the countryside.

"Nothing strange or out of the ordinary? Something, perhaps, that momentarily struck you as odd but then slipped from your mind?"

"I'm sorry. I just can't think of anything to help you."

He frowned for a moment, and then he shrugged. "Maybe we should go for coffee. But don't worry about the market. I'll arrange for the secretary in the police office to bring some in. Then we can talk more privately."

"Am I under arrest?"

"Oh, nothing like that." His gesture was quick and deprecating. "Just an informal chat, and as you pointed out, there aren't two chairs here, so why not use the *Policia National* at the municipal building?"

I never walked by the PN office without a shudder. The doorway was on the side away from the square, as if designed so those who entered would never be seen again. A sentry always sat slouched outside, a machine gun draped across his knees, his finger on the trigger. I could only hope the safety was on, that no inadvertent twitch would scatter my brains across the street.

"You must get very lonesome," Villa-Alba remarked after I had pulled my door shut and locked it. "Living here so far from home. I imagine the *inditos* do not make good conversation, since most of them are illiterate."

"You're right," I said. "It is lonesome. Sometimes I go for weeks without talking to anyone."

"But you do know some people in Palin," he said.

What did he know about me already? If he caught me out in a lie, he would never believe anything else I said. I could hardly demand to see a lawyer without looking suspicious. "But I haven't seen my lawyer," screamed the prisoner, just before the bullets of the firing squad ripped into his cranium.

"The schoolteacher comes over sometimes. He's *civilizado*." Maybe I could appeal to his Ladino prejudices.

"The schoolteacher," said Villa-Alba. "I've heard of the schoolteacher, but I didn't know he knew you."

That had to be a lie. In a town the size of Palin, everyone would know Guillermo came to my house. Better to say as little as possible and play dumb.

What could Simone have told them if they had captured her? What might Guillermo have said to her? Given his penchant for exaggeration, he could have made himself sound like Che Guevara. He might not even have mentioned my name.

We turned the corner. Down the street, the sentry at the doorway of the police office was standing erect, his gun at the ready. Villa-Alba must be somebody important if he impressed the guard so much. It was hard to keep my steps steady as I walked down the block, wondering if I would be driven to some isolated gully and shot.

Villa-Alba chattered on as if he were enjoying our time together. "Very warm at this altitude," he said. "Most gringos prefer to live higher up. What made you choose Palin?"

"It's about halfway up in the climatic zone I'm studying. It lies on the main road to the capital. If I need supplies, I can get them there."

"What kind of supplies?" He was on me again. Did he expect me to blurt I'd bought five kilos of explosives two weeks ago?

"Preservatives, mostly. I didn't want bottles to break and smell up my clothes when the baggage handlers threw my luggage off the plane."

"Some preservatives can be quite volatile," he remarked. "Be careful how you handle them. You don't want to blow up the police station."

We'd reached the doorway, a single opening in the blank, concrete wall. The sentry stood even taller than before. Villa-Alba stepped back to let me pass.

"It's the first door on the left," he said. With surprise, I realized that he didn't want to let me see any farther into his headquarters than I wished him to get into my house. It was this hope that sustained me. We were both men with secrets, he and I, and even if he dragged me off to torture me, he would have to let me into his private world if he wanted to learn about mine. His careful English and his genial language were an expression of the man he wanted to be – a cultured defender of the status quo. Does anyone want to grow up to be a brute? I realized I had something he could never aspire to. I lived on the normal side above the line, and he would forever be a creature of the dark, violent world beneath.

I didn't really know what I expected to find when I turned from the hall. To be honest, images of the rack flashed through my imagination, but all I entered was a barren room, its walls painted institutional green, furnished with a single metal desk, a battered file cabinet, and two wooden chairs. Villa-Alba and I were alone. Maybe the good cop-bad cop routine would come later.

"May I smoke?" I asked, struggling to keep my hand from shaking as I reached for the pack of Belmonts in my shirt pocket.

"Of course," he said. He was on home ground now, looking the police department equivalent of suave, as he held out a Zippo lighter to me. "I picked it up in North Carolina. It's hard to get flints for it here, so I have friends in your embassy bring some down each time they travel home."

I wondered how long he would string this out.

"When I met you in Tecpan," he said, "I didn't know who you were. I hope you didn't find me impolite."

"Not at all," I said. What else could I say? You are the politest spy I ever met?

"All kinds of people come to this country. Tourists, drug dealers, people interested in stealing ancient artifacts -- they all require a good deal of watching."

"So, your job is to watch me watching moths."

"But I didn't know it was moths you came to watch. When I encountered you with the young woman, all I knew was that you were associating with, shall we say, certain types of people."

"Priests and nuns? You can hardly find better people."

"Some of these priests like to stir up trouble. Two years ago, some Maryknoll fathers were caught in contact with the guerillas."

"I don't think the people in Tecpan are revolutionaries. They just came down here to help the Indians."

Even as I said these words, a craven voice whispered inside my brain. "If you defend the priests, then he will think you are a communist too. The church might protect them; it doesn't even know who you are." To my eternal shame, I artlessly added, "At least, I never saw or heard anything to make me think they were communists. I was only inside the mission for a few days.”

“And you didn’t hear them speak of any strangers? Anyone whose presence might seem out of place?” Villa-Alba was clearly down to business now.

“Strangers?”

“Let me come to the point,” he said. “Have you, at any time on your walks in the forest or at the mission, seen a man who might be of Chinese extraction?”

“Chinese?” I was baffled.

“The people in Tecpan might have spoken of him in passing. You might know him by his name or by a code name,” said Villa-Alba, with the look of a man who is playing his trump. “We have reason to believe he is called Yah-Zee.”

I exploded into laughter. The accumulated stress of the walk to his office, Villa-Alba’s intimidating cheerfulness, the uncertainty of knowing whether I was being arrested, on my way to die, burst forth in embarrassingly loud guffaws. I writhed on my chair; my hilarity intensified by the startled expression on Villa-Alba’s face. He must have set up this moment in his mind, prepared to see me blanch and crumble. Now he could only stare in dismay.

“Oh dear,” I said, wiping my eyes as the last fit of giggles died down. “Yah-Zee is a dice game for children. It’s not a person.”

“Our sources of information are extremely reliable,” he informed me in a chilling tone. It occurred to me this must be a moment of extraordinary humiliation for him, and it wasn’t in my best interest to embarrass him further.

"Perhaps someone suggested using it as a code name," I said, trying to keep a straight face with only partial success. Was I smirking at him? "I mean, revolutionaries don't go by their own names. You yourself said it might be a pseudonym."

His forehead wrinkled. Probably he was unfamiliar with the term pseudonym. "You will find revolutionaries who aim at world domination have a very limited sense of humor," he said. I restrained the impulse to suggest the secret police don't either.

The phrase "world domination" clanged in my brain. He must have read the telegram from Simone. It would be easy enough for him to intercept it. She would have handed in the text at the same municipal building in Tecpan where Villa-Alba had headquarters.

"Perhaps the use of Yah-Zee was a sort of strategy," I said in a helpful tone. "A red herring to divert suspicion from others." At least I hoped my tone sounded helpful.

"Herring?"

"It means a false scent, a diversion."

There was nothing I could do to relieve the absurdity of the situation. I had been hauled off to the police station only to find myself trying to restore the shattered ego of my persecutor. I suppressed the impulse to lean forward and give him a consoling pat on the shoulder. I thought maybe if I pretended to still be afraid, it might help-, but I couldn't think of anything else to say. A silence ensued and the longer it lasted, the harder it became for either of us to break it.

"May I go now?" I asked.

"Yes, of course," he said. "You know I just wanted to have you down here to give you some private advice."

I stood up. "Advice?" I echoed, feeling stupid.

"Gringos come to Latin America and forget they aren't in their own country. They shout at vendors in English and expect them to understand. They walk around thinking they can say and do whatever they like, and nothing will happen to them. The treat us the way they treat Mexicans in Texas, as if we were born to serve them, and they think that whatever they do, they will be protected just because they are from the United States. They run out of money or they get thrown in jail and they call the embassy and say, 'These spics are giving me a hard time, get me home now.' They think the cavalry will ride to their aid and they'll be back in their suburban homes the next day with nothing but an adventure to tell their kids."

"I'm not like that," I said.

"Well, just remember this. This is my country, and if you shit on me here, nobody can save you."

I was frozen in place. What terrified me was the sense that I had won a victory over him, however absurd and unintentional. He could never forget the humiliation. When he had ushered me into the room, he displayed the self-assurance of a man who has played a game many times before. He knew he would question me, intimidate me and break me. I would cling to shreds of self-respect for a little while, and then I would capitulate like all the others. Now he looked like a fool, and the fact that I alone knew how mistaken he'd been made my position seem all the more perilous. If he eliminated me, no one would know.

I cleared my throat. "I have to leave town tonight to continue my research."

He looked up at me. "Yes?"

"I mean... I thought... Well, in the movies people are always saying you're not supposed to leave town without telling them."

"We're not in a movie. I know how to find you."

"I'll be going then." I almost offered to report any Chinese I saw on the mountainsides as a way of sounding helpful but realized in time he would think I was mocking him. I walked into the hall and looked out the front doorway into the blazing glare of the street.

Could this be some kind of a trick? Maybe when I was halfway to the corner, the guard would shoot me in the back. Killed while trying to escape from routine interrogation. Or I might simply disappear. Captured, perhaps, by the guerillas known to be in the area on the very evening after the police had warned him of the danger. A tragic victim of the ongoing pattern of violence in the country and his own naiveté. The guard looked up at me as I appeared in the doorway, but his dark, Indian face with its broad cheeks and almost oriental eyes showed neither surprise nor interest.

"*Ya se va?*" "You're going?" he asked, his voice bored, almost listless. If my quick departure amazed him in any way, he didn't display it.

"*Me voy,*" I said. It was a routine pleasantry, but I had never seen any sentry speak to anyone.

Everything seemed to have meaning to my terrified mind. What did it mean that he was speaking to me? Was I really getting away from Villa-Alba? I quelled the impulse to dash around the corner to safety, walking with an awkward and measured stride. I was certain at any moment I would feel the shock of a bullet knocking me to the ground.

I thought when I stepped around the corner and out of the line of fire, I would feel secure, but as soon as the walls shielded me from view, my panic increased. Should I go to see Simone and warn her of Villa-Alba's suspicions? Would such an action bring my own safety in doubt? I was a fool to think he would just have me shot in the street. If he had wanted to do something, he would have come at night when there might be no witnesses. I had to leave the house. I would be crazy to leave the house. It would be an admission of guilt, probably a test on Villa-Alba's part. Maybe Villa-Alba didn't know very much at all, was just suspicious and using me to scare the priests out of the country.

I had to contact Simone and warn her. I couldn't contact Simone. The mission didn't have a phone and any telegram would be read as soon as it reached Tecpan. I should send somebody. Who could I send? Not Guillermo, that was certain.

When I opened the door to my house, I expected to see the place ransacked, but nothing had been moved. Maybe it was all in my mind. Maybe I was just projecting all my fears onto Villa Alba. I pushed back my only chair into a corner of the front room and sat with my back to the wall, waiting for army commandos to come storming in.

Even as I type these words now, years later, a faint echo of the terror of those next four hours makes my fingers tremble on the keyboard of my computer. It would be pleasant to say what I felt was fear for Simone, but it was simple panic. My first impulse was to get in the Scout, drive to the airport, and fly to California. I wouldn't even pack my notes. I hated research anyway. I'd lose my draft exemption, of course, but there were thousands of men going underground every day. A life without MacElwain wouldn't be bad. The man was an absolute prick.

I patted my pocket and felt the keys, only to realize I had just fifteen *quetzales* in my wallet. I had about two hundred in the bank in Guatemala City and the next check from my fellowship wouldn't be deposited for a week and a half. I could call my parents from the airport, get them to charge a ticket on their American Express card. I would get them to charge a ticket Simone and me. We could both fly to Berkeley and join a commune. I could save her from the stupidity of those priests.

In the third hour, I began to settle down and plan rationally. The important thing was to make my actions look as normal as possible. I would get the Scout at dusk, the way I always did and drive out of town toward the volcano. Then I would double back through the coffee fields on a narrow farm road. I'd know within a few minutes if I were being followed, because no one traveled there in the evening. If I saw anyone, I would turn up the highway and lose them in Guatemala City. If no one came, I would descend to the coast and take the road from Esquintla to Antigua. I could send a telegram in the morning. There were so many tourists in Antigua one gringo more or less would not be remarked upon.

At six o'clock I carried a tray of collecting bottles to the Scout. No one in sight. At the *gasolinera,* there was nobody loitering as I topped off the tank. Once I was out of town, I knew Villa-Alba couldn't stop me before I got to Antigua. For the first time since the knock on the door, I began to feel in control, almost clever.

At seven the next morning I handed in my telegram at Antigua, chortling at the cleverness of a text I was sure Villa-Alba's men could not decipher. "The Purified Water Lady requests the pleasure of meeting you three tables to the left of the tail you raised the first time we met. Be there Friday at 11:30 AM."

CHAPTER 12

"I'm jealous," said Simone. "All I get to do is deliver a few crummy posters to a house in Zone 2. You get interrogated by the secret police. It's not fair."

She leaned back and lovingly exhaled a stream of cigarette smoke toward the ceiling. In the protective gloom of the El Vaquero, it seemed as if she were spinning a protective cocoon of security around us. I'd arrived at eleven and waited, drumming my fingers and nursing a beer. I wanted to be as alert as possible when she came. I knew this wouldn't be easy.

Once she arrived, everything began to go wrong. I wasn't alone anymore, so the danger didn't seem as frightening as it had before she walked in the door. As I told her about the interview with Villa-Alba, she'd become star-struck with admiration, pouring on me the uncritical, positive regard she'd directed at Guillermo. Warmed in the spotlight of her affection, it was impossible not to luxuriate in Villa-Alba's embarrassment.

"It wasn't as much fun as it sounds," I said. "I was scared shitless."

"How could it be better? The guy hauls you in and falls right on his butt. I would have given anything to have been there. Yah Zee, son of Fu Manchu, has come to Guatemala to pursue the yellow race's revenge. You should have played along with him. How about Pa Chee Zee, his sidekick? You could tell him to foil their plan to put a double block on every road in the country. I bet he couldn't wait to put that in a report to the CIA. Let's have a couple more Gallos and start making up stuff for the next time." She waved to the waiter.

"Simone, do you have any money? I spent everything I had on the hotel room last night."

"I've got fifty *quetzales* at least. My mother sent a check down for Christmas and it only arrived a week ago. Padre Ramon cashed it for me before I caught the bus."

"Why did you say you were coming to the capital? "Just that I wanted some blue jeans and had to go shopping. A little white lie. It brings me up to eighty-nine. I can't wait to get to a hundred so I can blow him right out of the confessional."

"I'm not sure he'll be surprised. I suspect priests have heard it all."

"Well, we better get on it quick so we don't get upstaged by Father Mike. He looked guilt-stricken this morning. I'm not sure he can hold out for another week."

"Guilt-stricken? He may be the most amazingly moral person I ever met. What has he got to be guilty about?"

"Stupid," she said. "Why do you think I came to your room the first night instead of having you come to mine?" "You like to go to people's rooms? I don't know. I never thought of it."

"I was afraid you'd run into Father Mike. I'm sure he sneaks into Patricia's room once he thinks everybody is asleep."

"My God! What kind of mission are you running there? Who's Padre Ramon sleeping with? Maria? The dog?" I was delighted.

"Don't be crude, Jim. You just have to understand. It's hard for priests when they come to Guatemala. They're used to being surrounded by the church. Everywhere there are doting, middle-aged ladies who think they can do no wrong and want their sons to grow up to be just like them. Out here it's all different. The Indians don't care what they do because they're so grateful the priests don't look down on them like the Guatemalans do. A priest here can do anything. So they do."

"You never cease to amaze me. How you can buy into all of this is just beyond my comprehension."

"I believe because it is true."

Whoops. The old fear that by saying one wrong word I might lose her flickered back into my mind. The thought was larger, more frightening than any torment Villa-Alba could threaten.

"So, do you want to go to a movie?" she asked. "I saw a marquee for *Butch Cassidy and the Sundance Kid* as I walked down *Sexta Avenida*."

I gulped at my beer. "Simone, we've got to talk. You have to get out of the country. Villa-Alba thinks you're a spy; he thinks the whole mission is a nest of communists."   "Isn't it wonderful?"

"Simone, this isn't a game. You have to go back."

"Back to Tecpan? I just got here."

"Back to the United States, you idiot. We've been incredibly lucky Villa-Alba let me go. We have to get out of here. I'm going to get my parents to wire me money for tickets back to the States. We can go to Berkeley and live there."

She reached out and stroked my cheek. "Jim, you're so sweet."

"I'm not sweet. I'm just somebody who wants to keep you alive. And I want to keep you alive because you're good in bed, okay? I like it when I've held back as long as I can and I know I can't anymore. If you don't go with me to Berkeley, I'll be stuck masturbating for the next three months and you know it's a sin. You have to come with me."

"I love it when you try to talk dirty. That's something Tommy never could do."

"Screw Tommy. This is about us, Simone."

"The movie starts at one. We'd better get going."

"Come to California with me, Simone. We don't have any choice."

"That's because you're a Protestant and believe in predestination. We Catholics have free will morning, noon, and night. And right now, my free will is taking me and you to see Paul Newman. After I've looked into his blue eyes, we can talk."

She stood up and looked down at me as I sat hunched with my elbows on the table. "For Christ's sake, Jim," she said. "You've got to focus on the important things in life. What's important is being young and having a good time. If you cling to life too much, all you end up is old. That's what Christ teaches us, just live, that's all. That's what he meant about the lilies of the field."

"I thought *Lilies of the Field* was a movie starring Sydney Poitier."

She bent down and kissed me. "You're hopeless. It's why I love you. Come on, we'll go to the movie and then we'll go to the Panamerican Hotel and you can be my gigolo."

I went to the movie with her, walking along the sidewalks crowded with vendors selling cigarettes and lottery tickets and Chiclets, and sat with her on the empty benches of the second-class balcony. She bought two bags of peanuts spiced with chili powder and presented me with one as if she were taking me on a date. I put my arm around her as the lights went out, feeling like a fourteen-year-old out with a cheerleader. The song about raindrops falling on my head and Paul Newman cavorting on the bicycle was just the sort of thing Simone would love.

My hope of persuading Simone to return to the United States, which had disappeared in the El Vaquero, began to be reborn. We would go to the Panamerican and we would make love more wildly and passionately than ever before. I would be so jovial, so dashing, so affectionate she wouldn't be able to bear the thought of separation. Afterward I would tell her I had to go, that she had to come with me. In my fantasy she resisted at first, but she agreed in the end because she had to, because she couldn't live without me. Love would save her, not some sappy Christian self-sacrifice, but the joy of our bodies coming together. She would agree to Berkeley.

The Panamerican was hardly the scene for a Dionysian frolic. The elaborately carved doors opened onto an enclosed atrium filled with the dark polished wood tables of the restaurant. Each room had louvered doors like something out of the movie Casablanca. Plump, middle-aged Indian women in flowered blouses served as waitresses, and the maître d sported a gray moustache worthy of a veteran of Zapata's peasant army. The desk clerk was an elderly man in a dark suite who recorded our tourist card numbers without giving any indication he noticed the last names were different. "You have bags?" he asked in English.

"They're in the car," said Simone. "We'll get them later. We just thought we'd freshen up before seeing the cathedral."

I nudged her foot and she turned a giggle into a cough.

"Three twenty-one," said the clerk, handing over the key and gesturing toward the stairs.

"How polite," Simone said. "He didn't ask us to pay in advance."

"Not so polite," I said. "Three twenty-one is two floors up and directly across the way. He'll be able to check on us any time we come and go."

"I said he was polite. I didn't say he trusted us."

We reached the second balcony and walked across to our room. I stifled the urge to look back down at the desk clerk and fumbled with the key. Simone walked to the railing and looked down.

"There's a bald head eating turkey right below us," she reported. "There was a time when I would have killed to have a water balloon in a place like this."

"When you were very young, of course," I said, finally getting the door open.

"I think I'll stay young until I'm seventy-eight" said Simone. "Then I'll age overnight into a crotchety old bat. I'll carry a cane and if anyone dares to say, 'seventy-eight years young,' I'll smack him over the head with it. Maybe I'll put lead pellets in the tip, just to carry extra weight."

"The door is open, madam," I said. "Enter at your own risk. And may I say how glad I am you haven't taken up the cane yet."

Once we were inside, the mood darkened. The light from the frosted glass window suffused the room with a shadow-free pallor, turning the dark, Hollywood style bed into an antique monstrosity. An enormous spare bureau lurked in the corner. Cheap lithographs of Indian women peered down on us like the chorus from a Greek drama. My palms started to sweat and my mouth got dry. What if our carefree rendezvous became tawdry and uninspiring?

I think Simone felt it, too, because she sat primly on the edge of the bed and smoothed a hand along the coverlet. There didn't seem to be anything to say. I was overwhelmed by the immensity of the task I had set for myself, to reach out and touch her so intimately that she would lose all power over her life and follow me wherever I would go. What had I been thinking of in the theater? The first time I had slept with her, the intensity of my deprivation had carried me to her on a wave of pure lust. When she arrived in Palin, she had appeared so soon after the telegram there was no time to anticipate. This time felt different.

"You're certainly not the gigolo type," said Simone. "Maybe if you poured Wesson oil on your hair you could bring it off better."

"Simone," I began, "I don't want to just play games."

But of course, I was playing the most important game of my life. I was playing Love Me or Else, and if she didn't what could I do then? It was lunacy to think I could touch her perfect body with my mind, like Suzanne in the Leonard Cohen song. Still, I had to make her come with me. I reached out and stroked her shoulder.

"Why are you acting like a love-struck teenager?" she asked. "Your face looks absolutely sappy."

"Maybe it's because I love you," I said. "I want to make love to you. I want to be with you. I want you to come with me."

I pulled her to me and gave her a really classy kiss, just like in the movies. It was a pretty great kiss, but it didn't seem to make her will melt away.

"You may not be Robert Redford," she said when we came up for air, "but you'll do until he comes along. Help me unhook my brassiere."

I bent down to kiss her breasts and I could hear her heart thumping its healthy rhythm in my ear. She was so young and firm and alive that just for a second I could sense her indestructibility. In that moment, she could be all that mattered. We could live our lives concerned with nothing more than the daily drive to unite our bodies. The pulsing of our pleasure was so intense, that time, danger, fear were driven away. When we'd finished and lay in a sweaty embrace, I thought for one blissful instant I had succeeded, she could never resist the pleasure of sex with me.

"Come with me to California," I said. "I'll take you to Point Reyes. We'll watch the whales migrate and make love in the mist. We'll hike in the Sierras and screw under the pine boughs. We can go to Haight-Ashbury and watch the freaks on the street and sneak off and do it while we're high."

"Come with me to Altoona," she said. "You can thrill to the sight of the Horseshoe Curve on the Pennsylvania Railroad, play bingo at the parish church, attend the Juniata County Fair and watch the hogs get it on in the back pens."

"Simone, this is important. I'm offering you life. You could get killed here."

"You're offering me a dream," she said. "I could never go to California with you. How would we live there? What would I be? Some high school kid you picked up in Latin America. You'd hang out with your graduate student friends and talk about the university. I'd take pottery classes and try to look smart."

"You are smart. My friends would adore you."

"Your friends would look at me like a specimen. What would they say when they heard I'd gone to mass on Sunday?"

"They wouldn't care. It's a free country. That's what California means, doing your own thing."

"Not when your own thing includes belief in a Catholic God. They'd think I was, I don't know, bizarre. I've spent my life resisting my mother and the nuns who wanted me to be a nice Catholic girl. I'm not going to

California and have people try to liberate me into some hippy retread."

"You can be anything you want." I was indignant. "You're acting as if I am just another Purified Water Lady. I love you. They'd accept who you are."

"Remember what the Purified Water Lady said about taking things back from Guatemala, how they never look right in your living room? She was right. I wouldn't fit in in Berkeley."

"You could go to school. It's great being a student at Cal. The campus is beautiful, the professors are the best in the country. There are all kinds of people hanging out on the campus. There's the People's Park and weirdos on Telegraph Avenue. It's the greatest place in the world."

"I'd never get into Berkeley. My SAT's were crummy."

"There are a ton of colleges, junior colleges too. The tuition is really cheap once you're a resident." "Oh, I'd love it. This is Simone. She's majoring in physical therapy at Dumbass Junior College. 'Tell us about your midterm, Simone. Did you get all the muscles in the lower back right?" I'd pushed too hard. She was angry, sitting up in the bed, pulling the sheets around her as if to protect herself from an attack.

"I'm sorry, Simone. We've just got to get out of here."

"I just want to be happy!" she blurted. I could tell she was close to tears. "I just want to be myself. What's wrong with me? First Tommy wanted me to run away with him and now you want me to run away too. It's stupid."

"At least we're not out for one-night stands," I said, trying to lighten the tone.

"Don't you know Guatemala isn't real? Nothing that happens here matters. It's like being on a cruise ship. You can go into anybody's cabin for the night and ball their eyes out and then go home and it never happened. Altoona's real. Berkeley's real. Guatemala's just a painted backdrop with people in costume."

"Simone, Villa-Alba is real. What he can do to us will really hurt."

There was a pause. For a second I thought she was considering what I said.

"Take me back to Tecpan," she said. From her tone, I knew there would be no more argument.

CHAPTER 13

Of all the afternoons of my life, that was the most gray. Simone dressed and went down alone to pay at the desk. I met her in the lobby and, without saying a word, we walked to the lot where I'd parked the Scout. The longer we didn't talk, the harder it became to say anything. We lurched through narrow streets clogged with traffic and smelling of diesel exhaust. I began to whistle tunelessly. She looked out the window without comment.

The checkpoint at the edge of the city was unaccountably empty and the traffic streamed through with only the slightest slackening of pace. I thought of Riguberto, probably dead by now, but I was so depressed it seemed as if he were the lucky one. I'd never felt so helpless, so much of a failure. There was no place to turn. My research was worse than worthless with huge gaps in the data. I had precisely enough results to anger MacElwain and ensure I would never get my degree, but not nearly enough to write a thesis any other faculty member would accept. Simone, petulantly staring at the scenery, seemed willful and dangerous – not nearly as wonderful had she had just an hour before. I had trashed my life for her, yet she persisted in playing games that could get her killed. A half dozen times on the way up the mountain, I turned to her and opened my mouth, thought better of my words, and stared once again into the winding pavement ahead.

The three extra weeks of the dry season since we had first passed this way had transformed the countryside from verdant growth into a terrain of crackling leaves and faded blossoms. Sometime in May the rains would come again. Until then the grasses would lie dormant, the cornfields would rustle in the wind. On the higher mountains, Indian men had begun burning the dried stalks to prepare the land for tilling. The faint, acrid smell that blew in the window of the truck might have been the cremation of all my hopes. I would die, I was sure, either here in Guatemala or on some jungle path in Vietnam after I lost my deferment.

"Well?" said Simone.

"Well, what?" I said, feeling faint pride at having waited her out.

"Well, aren't you going to say something?"

"What do you want me to say?"

"I want you to say you're sorry and you won't do it again."

"Do what again?"

"Idiot. If you say what, the argument will just start up all over."

"What?"

"All you do is say, 'I'll never do it again' and I say, 'That's OK, it was really my fault' and then we can make up."

"But what if I do it again?"

"Do what again?"

"Whatever I said I wouldn't do. This is absurd."

"No, it's just like the confessional. You tell the priest you won't do it again and he forgives you, and if you do it again, then you are contrite again and he forgives you again."

"Jesus Christ," I muttered, "One minute you're making love to me and an hour later you're the priest and I'm whispering to you through the grill."

"God loves to forgive sinners. That's why there's more joy in heaven over one sinner saved than over ninety-nine righteous souls."

"OK. I'm sorry I did it. I'll never do it again. Would you mind telling me what you're forgiving me for?"

"Better not. You'd just end up doing it again on purpose, and then it would be harder to forgive you."

She slid across the seat and nestled against my shoulder. I was nonplussed. She seemed childish and superficial. And what was the terrible sin for which I was forgiven? Trying to save her life? Proposing marriage? Hardly things one expects to be forgiven for.

"Simone," I said. "I love you."

"Three times. Now you're stuck with me for life."

"It was your life I was talking about."

"Would you get your act together and start making up?"

"OK," I said.

Another plot was forming as I spoke. Padre Ramon was the answer to my problems. I would get him to send Simone home. He knew about Guatemala. He'd see she was in danger. He was responsible for her. He'd have no other choice once I told him about Villa-Alba. Think how guilty he would feel if anything did happen. When she was safely back in Altoona, I could pack up

and leave. I would get a job teaching high school
biology. There was talk about changing to a lottery
system. Maybe I would draw a high number.

Padre Ramon met us in the main room. He was
stacking wood and paper into the fireplace, using about
three times what was necessary. It was no wonder there
were smoke smudges along the mantelpiece. It restored
my faith in the Germans. It had seemed out of character
for them to build a fireplace with an inadequate draft.

"Good to see you," he said with professional
bluffness. "I've been hoping for visitors. I love the
people around here, but the same faces get tiresome,
month after month."

"He just wants someone to play Clue," said
Simone. "It's his new passion."

"I'll tell you what," I said. "Why don't you take
the first shower and Padre Ramon and I will play a hand
of gin rummy."

I felt incredibly sly, proposing a two-person
game, getting rid of Simone so I could talk to him one to
one. Padre Ramon positively glowed and if Simone was
suspicious, I couldn't see it in her behavior.

"I've got a deck of cards in my room," he said.

"Maybe we should play there. We won't be in
Maria's way as she sets the table for dinner." How
quickly I had made myself at home. Three weeks before
I'd been shifting from foot to foot, anxious I'd reveal my
designs on Simone's body.

Padre Ramon looked surprised, then grunted.
"Probably a good idea. We can play on my desk if you
bring something to sit on." He turned and waddled off

down the hall. I retrieved a chair from the dining room and followed.

"The room was jammed with furniture and had a stuffy, unclean smell. The door banged against the corner of a wardrobe as we entered. Padre Ramon threaded his way between his desk and the bed with surprising grace, one hip grazing the corner of a bookcase, the other just missing a coverlet. It was hard to see how he could reach the shower without climbing over the footboard. Two pairs of shoes and his extra pair of *huarches* jostled one another at the foot of the wardrobe. He'd Scotch-taped Christmas cards on the walls with pictures of families lined up in front of houses, fireplaces, and on stairways.

"There were six girls and me in our family," he explained waving a hand toward the gallery. "I've got twenty-three nieces and nephews."

"Do you ever get to see them?" I asked.

"The Maryknolls send us home for a month every two years, so I travel around and spend a few days with each family. You know what they say about fish and visitors stinking after three days."

My mind went back to the five days I'd spent, only a few weeks ago. "I hope I didn't stay too long when I was visiting here," I blurted.

"Oh, that doesn't apply in Guatemala. Nothing is the same here." He brushed away my apology with a wave of his hand, as if he were waving an incense burner, and began digging in the desk drawer. "I ought to warn you. This deck doesn't have a ten of diamonds. It makes the strategy a little different. Cut?"

"I'll trust you."

He dealt the worn cards into two piles, his pudgy fingers working with smooth efficiency. I picked up my hand and started to sort it.

"You'll never win if you move your cards around like that," Padre Ramon said. "Any player worth his salt knows to look at the other person in gin. Once you catch whether he stacks from right to left or left to right, you can figure out what he's saving within a few discards."

"Padre, I'm stunned. You really take this game seriously."

"Just trying to put you off guard. Do you want the three? I'll pick it up and put down a higher knock card. I hate people who knock. Do you play that you have to have nine cards melded on a knock or simply that the total of your unmelded cards must be lower than the knock card?" He put down the nine of diamonds.

"Nine cards melded."

I picked up the nine and discarded a two.

"Must be saving nines," he said. "Since the ten of diamonds is missing from the deck."

"Padre," I said. "Simone has got to go back to the United States. She will be in grave danger if she stays in Guatemala."

"I figured you didn't really want to play cards," he said, discarding the queen of spades.

"A man from the Guatemalan police picked me up and questioned me the other day. He is interested in the mission. He thinks you might be spies."

"The Guats think all gringo priests are spies. They don't like us because we take the Indian's side. Did he make any threats to try and scare her off?"

"No, but this wasn't just any policeman. I think he's pretty high up."

"They all act as if they're high up. Probably just a local trying to have a little fun with you."

"What about those people who got machine gunned you told me about?"

"They were Indians. What they do with foreigners is throw us out of the country. A half dozen Maryknolls got the boot two years ago. Of course, they did meet with the guerillas and issue a statement calling for the violent overthrow of the government. Come to think of it, the order got them out before the government could act."

"Padre, this man won't wait for the church to act. These things happen all the time."

"Are you going to give me all the clubs? This is too easy."

"Padre, you have to send Simone home. You're responsible for her."

"One bad thing about being a priest," said Padre Ramon, his gruff voice assuming a mock philosophical tone that still couldn't hide his resentment, "is that everyone wants you to do their dirty work for them. The mothers want you to keep their daughters from losing their virginity. They send their boys to parochial schools in the hope we will beat them into being good. You want me to ship Simone back to Altoona. Her parents want me to keep her here so she can't be in Altoona. In the end it all boils down to power. You're trying to make someone do something they don't want to do and you can't. So, you call the priest. 'Come here, Father. Put your shoulder to the wheel. Make them do it and take the blame.' You know what priests are? They're the garbage men of people's souls. Whenever there's a mess, call the priest to get rid of the trash. Do you know why I came to Guatemala?"

It seemed to me it was a little off the point, but I could hardly say I didn't care. Before I could answer, he went on.

"I came to Guatemala because the Indians only want me to do one thing, to be a priest. If the rainy season is a month late in their hamlet, they come to me and they say, 'Say the mass. Make the rain come.' I go out. The shaman is there. I say the mass. He does his ritual. Sometimes the rain comes. They come to me and say, 'I have sinned.' I give them their penance and administer the sacrament. Their sins are lifted from their souls. It's all I can do. I don't engineer lives. If you can't convince Simone to return to the United States, it's not my job to do it for you."

"Then the blood is on your hands." I couldn't keep the anger from my voice.

"Gin," he said with venom, laying down his cards.

Nothing in his speech had touched me. I was overcome with the failure of my last attempt to save Simone. As I looked across the desk, I saw only a corpulent, aging figure who, in my skeptical rancor, I took to be a deviant. I was young then and had little experience of failure. Being weak, I had never been asked to do something I hadn't the power to accomplish. I knew nothing of the impossibility of changing other people's lives. The only reality was the Padre Ramon, for reasons I found incomprehensible, was crushing my only hope in life.

I was baffled, outraged by his refusal. I was willing to sacrifice my thesis, my career, my chance of staying out of Vietnam. I know it sounds odd today, but a man could prize his deferment above all things. It was my shield and my salvation. In an age without hell, Vietnam served as a substitute for eternal torment, never ending perdition. For the sake of my deferment, I had endured stultifying courses and the petty tyrannies of academic life. I had traveled to Guatemala to pursue, in solitude, my mindless nocturnal exercises month after month. All this would be thrown away simply because Padre Ramon refused to do his duty.

As I stumped back down the hall, I faced the end of all my hopes, the destruction of my only chance to salvage a life together with Simone, whatever kind of life it might be. There's nothing worse, I thought, than to do all you can and then fail. I was too young to know there is something much worse – the fact that life goes on, even after one has failed completely, and no one notices the difference. Then you must go on with everyone else, grinding through the hours as if all your efforts hadn't happened at all.

Maria was my first teacher. She was laying the extra place for me at the table as I stamped into the room. She looked at me with a mixture of boredom, familiarity, and disgust.

"*Buenas tardes*," she said, the simple courtesy of her greeting belied by the cynicism in her voice.
"You've come back then."

"Yes," I said.

"The Germans always gave me plenty of notice when they were going to have guests. I could prepare enough soup for everyone. Now I will have to leave the bowls half filled."

I was tempted to point out since the soup bowls returned to the kitchen untasted, this was hardly a major hardship. Adding one person to a party of five wouldn't make much of a dent in the amount each person received. I resolved to make this clear. I was still wrestling with the problem of talking fractions in Spanish when she continued.

"*Norteamericanos*," she said with some disgust. "They are not as good as the Germans. The Germans came and built all of this. Built it well; built it solid. They lived their lives the same way. Every day, dinner at the proper hour. Every Sunday, mass started exactly on time. If people arrived late, they were ashamed to come in. The Germans treated people with respect. They didn't laugh and joke and try to be the Indians' friends. They acted like true priests. The Americans come like a politician, shaking the hand of every drunk in the town square, forgiving everyone. Their rooms are a mess and there are things going on that should not be."

She gave me a glance and it struck me for the first time that the person who cleans a room must have a pretty clear idea of what went on the night before.

"They will leave and everything will be the same," she said. "The Germans were solid. When they were done, they had built the entire mission. Built strong to last. Americans come and go."

"But no one benefited from the beautiful mission but the priests." I was surprised, in that unpatriotic time, to find myself defending my countrymen.

Maria had reached the door to the kitchen and paused to look back at me. "The Americans will go," she repeated.

Her eyes swept over me with contempt. I felt humiliated, insignificant. Simone told me once that Maria cheated the priests on the household accounts. I bet she didn't cheat the Germans. The Americans were a target of opportunity, less than a part of the landscape, foolish and wasteful, useful only to be exploited and despised. Then it struck me that I was trying to be just what she had accused the priests of being – someone who comes and goes, leaving nothing behind, not even a memory.

Maria's disdain was still stinging when we assembled for dinner. Paula Marie and Patricia arrived at the last minute, back from a distant hamlet where they had been teaching knitting to a group of women. Patricia displayed the work, copied flawlessly from the designs in a craft magazine from Chicago. She was like a mother showing off the achievements of an eight-year-old.

"The women are so smart. They can just look at the picture and produce a perfect copy! We're going to ship their work back to the Montana diocese to sell and get the women some money of their own. The people in that hamlet are so good. It's just my favorite hamlet of all."

I looked at a baby blanket that showed a chalet snugly nestled among snow covered pine trees and thought of the flawless and complicated weavings the women made themselves. What had this woman thought, as she knitted away, never having seen snow in her life? Maybe she's heard of snow, I tried to think charitably. It was difficult to believe anyone in Montana would be willing to pay the shipping costs for something that could have been knitted next door.

"Jim's got the fantastic story to tell," Simone broke in. "There's this policeman who thinks we're in league with a Chinese communist guerilla named Yah Zee!"

I told my story and everyone laughed even though Simone had already given away the punch line. The soup had come and gone, and a dry, intractable hunk of beef arrived sitting on a bed of gummy rice. The conversation turned to Father Mike's plan to build a sawmill for the town, or maybe buy an ambulance to drive sick people to the hospital in the departmental capital. I excused myself to go to the bathroom, grateful my moment in the limelight had passed quickly. When I reached the great archway to the entry hall, I looked back at the table.

The five sat amiably chewing their unpalatable meat, jawing at one another with the easy familiarity of those who live together for an indeterminate period of time. There could be no surprises between them, for they understood the futility of deception in such close quarters. I remembered Maria's caustic glance and realized with embarrassment that Padre Ramon must be only too aware of Simone's visits to my room. For the first time, I understood the power of things unspoken, the tacit understandings that govern the lives of old married couples and lifelong friends. Simone had come to my room so I shouldn't stumble upon Father Mike, yet he must be awaiting her quick, young step to pass before he made his way down the passage. They returned their soup untasted to Maria who took her revenge by stealing from them, preparing elaborate explanations should a rendering of accounts ever be unexpectedly demanded. Ramon's table games, Father Mike's idealism, Patricia's scrubbed sincerity, Simone's brash peccadilloes were all the devices they needed to keep their society running.

In his twisted way, Villa-Alba had stumbled upon a great truth about the mission. Its inhabitants were conspirators, not in some clumsy, futile attempt to overthrow the government, but in an elaborate charade to deceive themselves. The circle around the table had joined together to deny what they all were – refugees from an America that had abandoned their God and the sterile pieties of religion. The Beatles, the hippies, and Richard Nixon brought no contaminating touch here among the Indians who had survived four centuries of conquest and domination. To that conspiracy they had sacrificed the right to speak the truth clearly to one another, the freedom to stretch their lives and grow to the fullest, subordinating their wills to an unseen and unfelt purpose.

The mission looked not out to the world, but in on itself, chaining its members in the lockstep of an elaborate minuet of faith, hope, and deceit. "In my father's house are many mansions," Christ had said when he called them to Him, and in this Teutonic fortress they made their abode, wrapped in His redeeming love, serving time like prisoners in a stockade until He came with their release. How could my simple bribes of love and passion, honesty and commitment persuade Simone to leave? I had been struggling all day to kidnap a baby from its parents, to rip and organ from the tissues of which it was a part. I turned back through the archway, accepting my defeat.

CHAPTER 14

By the time I returned to the table, the routine of the mission had reasserted itself, and the circle was deep in planning the next day's schedule. Father Mike would head for a hamlet in the mountains north of town. He would drop Paula Marie off at another knitting class on the way, but must be certain to return by four-thirty so she could attend a rosary before supper. Simone would go with Father Mike unless I was staying over another day. Their faces turned inquiringly toward me and I found myself with nothing to say.

"I hadn't really thought about it," I confessed.

Where could I go? I could hardly stay here, a perpetual guest under the Padre's roof. I could head for Guatemala City and California, but that would mean abandoning Simone forever. Whatever my relationship with Simone was to be, commitment was clearly not part of it. To go to Palin would be to walk back into the clutches of Villa-Alba, but more horribly, it meant returning to my research. In the jumble of fear and hope of the last few days, the abandonment of months of labor had gone unnoticed and, I realized, un-mourned. I had crossed a psychological Rubicon when I bolted from the village, and the thought of leaving my notes and collections to gather dust until the landlady threw them out when she reclaimed the house gave me a thrill of revenge. I could see Doña Felicia, the squat Ladina owner, clucking as she dumped them in the trash.

"I'll stay one more day and then I'll be leaving for the States," I announced. "I have to meet with my adviser to discuss the progress of my research," I added lamely, lest my sudden departure seem weird or out of character.

"Probably a good idea," said Padre Ramon. "When you're away from your home too long, the local politicians start to spook you."

I didn't bother to protest. I was overwhelmed with the intoxicating freedom my decision gave me. Never to gather another moth. Never to speak to MacElwain again. Maybe I could change my name on my return, get someone else's Social Security number, and work in a McDonalds for the rest of my life. By the time the draft board caught up with me, the war might be over. I could pump gas at night and surf during the daytime. I could go on the road like Jack Kerouac, write poetry, invent a better kind of snow cone, and make a million dollars.

"I thought your adviser was coming here over Easter," said Father Mike. "I was looking forward to meeting him. I find men of science often have a poetic turn to them."

"His wife was suddenly taken ill," I said. "But you're not missing much. I think MacElwain would have a hard time rhyming anything with thermal determinism. It's all he talks about."

"Intellectual rats preach verminism, but I prefer thermal determinism," suggested Simone. This kind of stuff was right up her alley. "But I thought," she continued wickedly, "you had told me your adviser was single."

"He was," I said, "but he married since I came to Guatemala."

"And his wife became sick," said Sister Patricia. "How sad."

"He knew she was ill when he married her," I said. "It's rather touching, really."

"Then why was he planning to come over Holy Week?" asked Father Mike.

"She's often OK for months at a time," I said (would the lies never stop multiplying?), "but then she has relapses." I could see Sister Patricia was about to ask about the exact nature of her illness. I was sorting wildly through diseases with appropriate symptoms when Padre Ramon came to my rescue.

"Simone, I almost forgot to tell you. You got a letter from Altoona. I left it on the table in the hall."

Simone jumped up and headed from the room. No matter how cool and detached one is, a letter from home has a magnetic quality. It is a message directed to you alone, with the forethought and detail a telephone conversation cannot match. I looked toward the doorway, expecting to see her reappear with the envelope in her hand, but apparently she was standing at the table as she read. I could picture her snatching the envelope open, racing her eye down the page.

The front door slammed.

"Did I hear a gasp?" asked Father Mike. "I hope it isn't bad news."

"Maybe we should go after her," I said, half rising from my chair.

"If it's bad news, better to let her be," said Padre Ramon. "People can be like wounded animals. They need to hide away and lick their wounds."

I hesitated. The ring of insincerity in his clichés spoke more of his inability to handle an emotional scene than an acknowledgement of a need for privacy.

I looked to Father Mike. "It's hard to know what's right at times like these," he said.

Sweet Jesus, I thought, does the priest's handbook contain a glossary of empathetic phrases? Anything would be better than listening to this. I stood up and left the room without comment. Maybe it was only my imagination, but I felt for just a second Sister's Paula Marie's idolatrous gaze had shifted from Father Mike to me.

Simone was outside on the street, leaning against the adobe wall, weeping. Her hands were balled at her sides. The tears ran down her cheeks like rivulets on a car window in the rain. Her shoulders pumped up and down as she gasped for breath, but her grief was almost soundless. When I put my arms around her, she pushed me away with a fierce, impulsive gesture, then collapsed onto my shoulder.

I had no idea what to say, so I patted her shoulder blade without saying anything. What could I say? It will be all right? I had no idea what she was weeping about. She nestled her body against mine, and, and I know this is going to sound bad, I was suddenly, terrifically aroused. It was the most intimate moment of my life. I felt tall and strong. I turned her face upwards and kissed her eyes. The tears tasted salty on my tongue.

My body was pressed all against her, and she, the divine child-woman, pressed back against me, quivering.

The sobs began to subside, coming in gusts like the trailing squalls of a thunderstorm. It was a great time not to talk, and for once, I was smart enough not to say a thing. I knew she would start the conversation in her own time, so I needn't risk being condescending or inappropriate.

"That stupid bastard," she said, the words dropping from lips heavy with her sorrow. "He had to go and get himself killed. First, he flunked out of Penn State just to piss off his mother and lost his deferment. Then he went to boot camp so his friends wouldn't think he was a coward. Now he's dead."

So Tommy was dead. For a moment, I felt guilty, remembering the jealous way I had pried for information when we were together in Palin. It was as if by wishing he had no tie to her I had guided the Viet Cong fire that smashed life from his body. He had a beautiful body, Simone had said, but his body was beautiful no longer. I was torn between curiosity to know more (how he died, where, what time of day, on what day) and the impossibility of asking. Simone probably didn't know anyway.

"Come on," I said. "There's still time to get a beer or six."

She laughed, more a short hiccup than a true laugh, and put her arm around my waist. "I warn you, I'm going to talk about him," she said.

"That's all right," I said. God, I felt empathetic.

"I know just the place to drink them," she said. "We can get loaded and look at the moon. I'll take you down the road where I sent the patrol looking for the guerillas that time."

The lighted doorway of the empty *tienda* reminded me for a chilling instant of the first time we met Villa-Alba, but the storekeeper dug a half dozen beers out of the cooler with a bland and impersonal air. Simone said he looked tense.

"Business OK?" she asked as I dug out my wallet.

"Like always," he said. "Since the violence began nobody wants to spend. Sometimes I wonder if it is worth my trouble to keep the store open at night."

"I'll come down every night," she said. "Maybe you will give me a free bag of Tor-Trix as a reward for being a steady customer."

"It's all right," he said. "And will you bring your friend? After all, he's the one doing the paying."

"He's leaving day after tomorrow. Then I'll be alone and sad."

"Maybe you should go with him," he said. "Then you wouldn't be alone."

"And you would have no business," she answered. "No, I have to stay here."

"I think she should come with me," I broke in, glad to have found an ally at least, if only a casual one.

"The *gringos* never stay," he answered. "We live here in the pueblo as our ancestors did and in the end they take us to the graveyard and our families come each Todos Santos to visit us. The foreigners come and go." I wondered if he had been talking to Maria.

"Anyway," said Simone, "I am staying here and I am going to get drunk. And then," and she turned to me talking in English, "I'm never going to think of Tommy again. Not once."

"Right," I said as I got my change from the store owner. "You have to go on." One more night of Tommy, I thought, and I'll be done with him. Maybe she'll follow me to California after all.

"It's not far to the place I have in mind," said Simone, "I could find it with my eyes closed."

This was no idle boast, for the new moon had already set. Most of the streetlights were not working. Smoke from the burnt fields hung in the air dimming the faint light from the stars. The trail was a ghost track through the stubble of old corn stalks. It wound up a low hillside to a fallow patch at the edge of the woods. The grass that invaded the plot was coarse, but sheep had cropped it as close to the ground as if it had been mowed. We inspected the ground for droppings, found an open spot, and Simone sat huddled with her knees to her chest as I prized the caps off with my pocketknife.

"I'll never know why Protestants are so fucked up," she said, her voice an idle and reflective aside.

"What do you mean?"

"You would think they have the perfect set up. You can use contraceptives when you have sex, no priests or nuns watching you, getting to go to public school with kids from the wrong side of the tracks. That's it. You can eat meat on Friday. The preachers walk around in regular clothes. They don't even use wine in communion. I snuck into church with Tommy once. He drove me all the way to Irwin and we sat in the last row. What a bore. They even brought the Communion to you on plates passed down the aisle, as if you were at a cocktail party. There was no miracle there."

"Didn't your mother wonder where you were?"

"Mom and Dad were visiting Aunt Catherine outside Ambridge. All hell broke loose that weekend. Patrick was supposed to look after the house, but he just took off with his friends and didn't get back until ten o'clock Sunday night."

"What about Tommy's mother?"

"I forget where she was. It wasn't like the old bitch to let Tommy out of her sight. Oh, I know. She had the flu and stayed in bed for days with a cold compress over her eyes. You would have thought she was near death. Tommy's dad was working day shift at the mill. I was terrified that someone would see us."

"Was Tommy religious?"

"No, he just said, 'Church is stupid.' It was about all he could do in the way of moral or intellectual discussion."

"Sounds as if you had a lot in common. He couldn't talk and you couldn't stop."

"Don't blame Tommy. If you had his mother, you wouldn't be able to talk either. She was the reason I wouldn't do it."

"Wouldn't do what?" It seemed to me as if there wasn't much Simone hadn't done with Tommy.

"Marry him, you dope. The minute she said, 'Of course, my Tommy will do the right thing' I knew there was no way I would let it happen. Nobody was going to do the right thing by me."

As we started our second beers, Simone's cockiness slipped away. She recounted her story with straight, spare phrases and, with the exception of Tommy's mother, little rancor.

She told me about the time she was sure she got pregnant one Sunday afternoon.

"It was when the sex was best. I would come from Mass with all my sins swept away, clean and pure as a virgin again. I couldn't wait until I got my hands on him. There was never any guilt on Sunday. It was like the first time all over again. It was my fault, really. I'd counted the days since my last period and I was sure I was safe. I told him he didn't have to use a rubber."

A month later, anxiety gave way to panic. One night she shared her fears with Tommy. "Big mistake. The idiot talked to his father, so of course his mother knew about it that night. I went over to see him the next day and found myself in the middle of a council of war."

I could imagine the scene. The family sitting together in a living room of sturdy, ugly furniture that Aunt Ella had left when she died. Good quality but impossible to sell. Tommy's father trying to be polite in a nervous, gentle way. Out of his depth. Tommy looking as if her were afraid he'd be sent to his room, quelled and dominated. The mother, silent and hateful, expecting Tommy's father to do the talking for her, but unable to keep from taking over.

"Tommy's mother acted upset, but she was really triumphant. I was the little slut who had stolen her boy, and now his life would be ruined. She had wanted him to go to college. He would be the first in the family, but that would be out of the question now that he had to support me. Not that she was excusing Tommy in any way, but…"

Tommy's mother looked at Simone as if she had been lurking behind lace curtains in a red light district waiting to ensnare her boy. But she had taken too long and Simone was ready for her.

"'I don't understand why this discussion is necessary,'" I told her. 'It was never my intention to marry your son. My only regret is that he seems to be unable to keep his affairs to himself.' I stood up, thanked Tommy's father for the Coke he had given me, and walked out. I should have known to go to Patrick first."

"Patrick?"   "Patrick knew just what to do. It turned out he'd already gotten an abortion for one of his girlfriends."

"I thought you hated Patrick."

"He was my brother. He knew what to do. He even came up with most of the six hundred bucks."

"What did your mother say?"

"Why did she need to know? Patrick knew that best of all. He arranged the excuse and everything. We said I was going to a theater trip to Pittsburgh with some girls from school. I didn't even miss a day of classes."

"She had to have known, Simone. No family is that good at keeping secrets. Did you confess it to the priest?"

"I waited until a visiting priest from Italy was down at Saint Marks and went there to confess. I'm not sure he understood what I was saying. How do you say abortion in Italian, anyway?"

"I suspect it's something like *aborto*."

"Well he couldn't have been too upset given the light penance he gave me."

"And Tommy? What did Tommy do during all of this?"

"What could Tommy do? He was no match for his mother. She arranged for him to spend a summer with an uncle in Ohio, then go directly to Penn State in the fall. It's funny. Usually it's the girl who gets packed off. Poor Tommy."

"Didn't your family pack you off to Guatemala?"

I honestly think Simone had never thought of it before, through it seemed obvious enough. Once stated, the idea had such power she had to resist it actively. If her parents had packed her off, her parents had to know. She was still young enough that it was important they not know.

"It was my idea to come to Guatemala. Nobody told me to go to hear the presentation by the missionary priest talk to the CYO. I looked at the slides and decided this was where I wanted to be."

"Your mother was against the idea?"

"Well, no, but it's because she always wanted me to be involved in the church. If she couldn't have a daughter who became a nun, this was the next best thing."

I had pointed out a path leading to dangerous ground. Simone was bright enough to look ahead and see what lay beyond the next turning, so she balked and turned back against me.

"Maybe it's a good thing you're going back to California," she said. "Maybe you're having a bad influence on me. My mother would say you are 'one of the wrong crowd.' She was always warning me against the wrong crowd. Mostly you could tell the wrong crowd by where they bought their clothes. No sense of quality, she would say, made of flashy, cheap fabrics. Though how she thought she was getting quality from JC Penney is beyond me."

"I don't like to think of myself as being in any crowd," I said, "but if I'm going to be part of a crowd, then the wrong one is the one for me. I've never bought anything at JC Penney. Why don't we both go back to Altoona? I'll wear tie dyed jeans. You mother will know I am to blame for all your straying."

"Oh James," she began, and her voice was more serious than I had ever heard. "You don't know what you're saying. They would do terrible things to you. They would take you to the Knights of Columbus picnics and talk about getting you a good job at the mill. They'd lure you into drinking matches until your potbelly hung over your belt. Your hair would thin, and you'd start combing it forward to cover up. You'd never be my wonderful, skinny, horny James again."

"Never," I said. "You won't let them."

Then, suddenly, she was crying. I wondered what I'd said. Maybe it wasn't something I'd said at all. Maybe it was just the grief of Tommy's death coming back to overwhelm her.

"I can't stop them. No one can stop them. They won't give up and they never quit because they know they're doing the right thing. That's why I can't go back. No one in the mission can. The priests can't face America again. They can't face the after-mass coffee klatches and the adoring fourteen-year-olds who call them 'Father What a Waste' behind their backs. How could Father Mike go back after what he's done with Sister Paula Marie?"

"Surely he could be forgiven," I said.

"Oh, they'll forgive his transgressions. That's no problem. The Mass is nothing but a car wash with parishioners trooping through and coming out with their souls glittering in the sun, a week's worth of crud washed away and a coat of wax to ward off future evil. What they can't forgive is where we've been. Away. Out on our own. Not needing people like them. They know we'll all go out again. Independence is an addiction like smoking or sex. Once you've experienced it, you want it over and over."

"But if it's true, why did your parents send you out here?"

Damn! Why did I have to blunder back to her mother? The woman was everywhere, looming like a ghastly apparition, menacing and awful. Why did I, only trying to be helpful, have to force Simone down the path into her past? If her mother knew, then Simone couldn't be a child any longer. If her mother had arranged for her to come out here, the Simone wasn't a young adventurer, she was an exile, banished from the world of youth, like an animal sent to a shelter, never to be spoken of again.

"Fuck you," she said, but her voice held no emotion. "Fuck Tommy. Fuck everybody. Go to California. I thought you were different, but you're just a tourist. Guatemala is quaint, to be looked at and commented upon, and appreciated. You come, you look, but you never touch anyone. Get in your air-conditioned bus and get out of my life."

She stood up, brushed the bits of grass from her back with an air of dignity and resignation, and walked away into the darkness. The suddenness of her departure left me sitting alone and startled, even though there wasn't a single hurried movement. She was out of sight by the time I collected myself and struggled to my feet, stumbling forward until I found the ditch at the side of the road. The dusty surface made a gentle, gray swath in the starlight. I explored my way around a curve and could see the lighted doorway of the store on the square. Somewhere ahead, I guessed, Simone was striding along, unseen, between me and the light. Funny, I thought, that the storekeeper should stay open so much later on a night with no business. If I could just catch up with her before she reached the mission, maybe we could make up the way we had before.

Villa-Alba and his squad were waiting in the shadows at the edge of town. "It's good to see you again," he said with exaggerated courtesy. "I'm so glad I had the opportunity to contact Professor MacElwain after our first interview. Otherwise the situation could be extremely embarrassing."

Simone was nowhere to be seen.

CHAPTER 15

"MacElwain?" I could only stutter in amazement. "How do you know MacElwain?"

"I don't know him," Villa-Alba replied with elegant coolness. He was savoring the moment. "I never heard of him until this morning. It's lucky for you I made inquiries with the American embassy as to your background. Otherwise your activities could have resulted in a great deal of trouble."

"My activities?"

"Luckily for you, nothing you did caused the death of a Guatemalan national. Lucky for you and me, I might add, since our government does not wish a confrontation with the embassy at this time. Your expulsion will satisfy our national honor, and, I hope, persuade the embassy it is imperative to consult before running operations. Making you a student of moths probably sounded like a good cover. Someone with an excuse to be in the jungle at night. You gringos love jungle operations. You think the whole country is one big jungle. You have an agent in Chimaltenango who's pretending to be building a factory for carved mahogany doors. He travels in the jungle looking for stands of timber. In three years, he hasn't exported a single door!"

"Operations?" All this was going far too fast for me.

"Your friend Guillermo was only too willing to cooperate and tell us about your activities. I bet you thought you were doing a wonderful job infiltrating the guerillas. I'll tell you something. The real communists knew Guillermo was a fool. I'm surprised you didn't see that." In the dimness, I saw Villa-Alba's lips tighten into a tense smile. He turned to the man beside him. "Put this one in the truck to the capital," he said. "He's a class one prisoner, but you don't have to be gentle."

"What have you done with Simone?" I asked as the man grabbed me and started pushing me down the road. "You bastard, what have you done with her?"

Villa-Alba turned his back and started toward the town, showing the men around him he had more important things to do than talk to a single gringo. I lunged after him, but the grip on my arm jerked me back.

"Where's the girl?" I shouted, my voice cracking is desperation. "She hasn't done anything. She was with me the whole time."

"*Lo siento*," someone behind me muttered sardonically, "but continued noise will compromise our operation." Efficient hands pinned my arms behind me, and a pair of handcuffs snapped around my wrists. They spun me around and pushed me toward an army truck lurking in the gloom. I stumbled and fell forward onto the road, unable to break my fall. Someone above me gave a short, reflexive bark of laughter.

I broke my nose when I landed. I could feel the blood gushing out onto the dust, taste it as they dragged me forward, as it dripped down my lip and onto my tongue. I gasped for breath, inhaling a suffocating mixture of dirt, blood, and snot. I began to cough, and then the coughing turned to retching as I struggled to free myself. They turned me over, and I found myself sitting, ludicrous, in the dirt with a circle of curious soldiers gathered around me in the gloom.

"In the truck," said the man who was apparently their leader.

I was lightheaded from my fall. The blood pouring from my nose drenched the front of my shirt. I started to rise to my feet, then fell back clumsily on my butt. The men stood around in the darkness, none willing to show any courtesy, but forbidden (I would later learn) from anything that might be construed as torture. I sat there, my nose burbling, as I tried to catch my breath.

"Lift him up," the leader ordered and one of the soldiers grabbed me by the arm. When I reached the back of the truck, he pushed me and I flopped forward again, landing not on the metal floor of the truck, but on the leg of another prisoner. Gradually I wedged myself upward until I was sitting, my face no less than a foot from his. He was an Indian in ragged clothes, badly beaten, but his dark eyes were alert.

With our faces so close, as close as lovers about to kiss, there was an almost irresistible urge to say something, but what to say? My schoolbook Spanish allowed for only the most formal phrases of greeting – so pleased to meet you, how is it going with you? The swelling under his left eye, the cruelly scuffed skin along the side of his neck made it clear Villa-Alba had not suggested anyone be gentle with him.

"Gringo?" he asked, his voice cracking with the pain that had been done him.

"*Si*." I nodded vigorously, as if he couldn't understand even this, the simplest of words.

He shrugged, but didn't add anything.

"Have you," I asked, talking slowly and loudly, like on of the idiotic tourists who seem to think all foreigners are deaf, "Have you seen a *gringa* girl tonight?"

He looked at me uncomprehendingly. "*Una gringa?*" he echoed.

"Yes, with long brown hair…" I started to gesture but the hand cuffs brought me up short. "With long brown hair worn, uh, uh." I wanted to say worn loose but my Spanish failed and I lapsed into silence.

"*Una gringa?* Today?"

"Yes, today, I mean tonight. In the last few minutes."

"She wasn't a *gringa*."

"Who wasn't?" I was beginning to lose him. I could hear his words starting to blur.

"*No hay gringas aqui.* No gringas here."

"Who were you talking about then?"

He just shook his head. I wanted to grab him, shake him. I was sure he had seen something.

"Silence!" One of the soldiers must have been left to guard the truck. All I could see in the darkness was the glowing ash of a cigarette.

"*Es jodido,*" the man muttered. "It's fucked up." He slurred his speech like a drunkard. In a minute he had either fallen asleep or passed out and was slumped against my shoulder. I strained to hear what I could, but his labored breathing roared in my ears.

The shots rang out about fifteen minutes later, flat cracks of rifle fire coming in a ragged volley, followed by screams of pain and voices begging in

Spanish and Mayan. Another volley followed and by the third round the firing became so irregular it seemed to lose all organization. The screaming reached its highest pitch after the third volley. Next came the moaning, low tortured groans beyond horror, sheer pain that called out without words, as an animal might cry in its torment. It just went on and on. The shooting tapered off, like the last drops of a storm falling in random clusters on a roof.

Was Simone out there? There was no way to tell one voice from another, no way to separate one speaker from the common babble of pain and despair. I knew little of weaponry, the guns could be firing a few yards away or a mile. Maybe they were so far Simone couldn't have been dragged to them. Maybe she was in another truck, and would be dumped together in some jail and rescued by the embassy. My mind rushed to create possibilities as I sat there, braced against the weight of the slumped man. No matter how fast I thought, underneath all of my frenzied invention, lay the cruel substrate of certainty. Simone was dead.

The motor on the truck cranked and, almost before it caught, the unseen driver popped the clutch and turned onto the road. With the lurching motion, my companion slumped down and back, his head resting against the tailgate of the truck. He must have been in pretty bad shape, because, despite the bumps in the road bouncing his head against the metal barrier, he didn't stir. After about an hour, he had a bowel movement, and then he died. So I rode in a stinking haze onward into the night.

The blood from my nose had clotted into a crusty mess down my chin. I licked my lips to clean them, and the salty tang of my blood was refreshing on my tongue. If nothing else, it was proof I was alive.

They don't shoot gringos, I told myself, if nothing else the newspapers would have a field day. They just hauled Simone away in another truck. It's what they do. They divide you up when they want to question you. They'll expel her from the country. Maybe they'll pitch out all the priests in the mission. That's all that will happen.

I repeated this mantra to myself for three hours as the wheels of the truck thrummed steadily down the Panamerican Highway. I hope it doesn't seem as if I am affecting bravado, but I can honestly say that the fear for my own safety had absolutely left me. As I persuaded myself Simone must be safe, then I must be safe as well because I was alive and breathing. A terrible massacre had happened, I thought, with the comforting security that a terrible thing hadn't happened to me.

The truck stopped and started, making turns after some halts, and light from streetlights filtered around the flap at the back. I began to look forward to the end of the trip when I would see Simone again. Next the truck lurched to the right, stopped, and the glow from the streetlights disappeared. I could hear the squeaking of a door being pulled shut. Then there was nothing but darkness and the idling of the truck. If they don't turn it off pretty soon, I remember thinking, the carbon monoxide is going to kill us. Then the motor shut off, steps retreated, and I was left in the quiet darkness.

I guess I must have overestimated my own importance, or maybe I just didn't comprehend the military penchant for wasting time, but I honestly thought a squad would come out to escort me to my cell. They would be men with well polished boots, like the SS in a move about World War II. Someone would guard me and the other prisoners until someone else, a consular official or an attaché, would come from the embassy. There might be embarrassing questions, and then I would be released.

After fifteen minutes, I realized I had to go to the bathroom. It also struck me that since my legs weren't shackled, I might be able to move around. Maybe I could slip out through the garage and make it to the embassy on my own. On the other hand, I didn't want to be shot escaping. Maybe I should wait for the attaché, by now an efficient official with the flawless language school Spanish, a bit of a twit, actually, who would come wielding the power and influence of the United States to rescue one of the nation's own. I edged silently toward the tailgate, rose to a crouch to get my leg over it, and tumbled on the cement of the garage, landing on my right shoulder.

Once I wedged my way to my feet, I could see the garage was not a dark as it seemed when I was inside the truck. The room was huge, big enough to hold twenty vehicles, and empty except for another truck, like my own, parked about five spaces away. A naked bulb burned at each end, leaving the center in twilight gloom. The garage doors had once had windows, several of which were now missing their glass. A lighted hall led from the far end beyond the other truck. On one wall stood a long line of shelves, filled with wrenches, vice-grips, screw drivers, and boxes of spare parts.

I was stupid to worry about urinating. With my hands behind my back, couldn't unzip my fly. I might as well have let myself go sitting in the truck. To judge from the smell of stale urine, would not be the first to relieve himself there, but at least the others could take aim at the wheel of a truck. For some confused reason, I moved toward the other truck, though what I was hoping to find, I have no idea. Finally, I let go, shuddering with disgust as the warm rush spread down my pants leg.

Still, with release came relief. The painful urgency left and, despite the revulsion at my wet pants, I felt one of my problems was solved. With my legs straddled like some absurd cowboy, I made my way to the back of the other truck. The canvas flap hung slightly open. I got a knee on the rear bumper, wedged the other beside it, and with the gentleness of a puppy nuzzling its way to its owner's lap, I pushed my face forward into the gloom.

All that was left of Simone lay before me, her head almost directly below my chin. Her body looked all wrong, like clothes cheaply packed with padding, arms and legs ludicrously askew. She lay on her back, looking up with a blank expressionless stare at the canvas top above her, her tongue half protruding through her teeth. Her jeans were drenched in blood. She still had a barrette in her hair, but someone must have stolen her wrist-watch and, curiously enough, her shoes.

She was alone in the truck, borne in state to the capital where the destruction of half the populace was so casually planned. No dignity, no catafalque to support her remains; just a life, like that of my companion in the other truck, which had ended too soon. I stared at her with a dry, curious intensity, trying to see if there was fear remaining in her face, wondering if she was abused before she was shot, but there was no trace of humanity left in her. The callous bullets which, without compunction, had torn her belly, had driven the soul from the body with a ruthless ferocity.

I was too tired for grief, or anger, or even despair. For the first time in my life, I realized how men could believe in the existence of a soul. Her body was there, but Simone was gone. Lying there, inert, abandoned, on the harsh metal floor of the truck was nothing I had loved, or touched, or shared. It was just a carcass, nothing more. Yet I couldn't leave her. I crouched there, with my ass hanging out of the back of the truck and my face next to hers, my eyes roving over every detail for I knew I would never see her again. I was neither revolted not entranced, I just lingered on.

A hand gripped my shoulder, firmly, not roughly, and pulled me back from the truck. My feet touched the concrete, my legs buckled, and I found myself seated, looking up at a circle of men around me, staring down with professional detachment. MacElwain was there, and an American in a light summer suit with a conservatively striped tie, and several Guatemalans in open necked uniforms. Villa-Alba was not among them.

MacElwain spoke with an authority I had never heard before. "Come with me," he said. "We've got to get this straightened out."

CHAPTER 16

He turned and walked toward the end of the garage. The man in the summer suit reached down and took my elbow.

"I'm Michael Furnival, assistant counsel at the embassy," he said, as if he were introducing himself at a cocktail party. "If you'll come this way, I think we can get your case straightened out."

He tugged at my arm, but I made no motion to rise. I sat on the grimy floor and stared at him, my mouth hanging open. Even though he was pulling on my forearm, I could hardly believe he existed. He looked so clean and his fingernails were clipped evenly. There wasn't a wrinkle in his tie, or his shirt, or his forehead. Innocence radiated from his pleasant face. He was a bank manager, perhaps, transported by an alien beam and appearing miraculously out of place.   "Come on," he said, pulling harder. I remained on the floor, feeling the oil left by some ancient, mistreated engine soaking into the seat of my pants. All the grief and exhaustion swept over me and I began to weep, without making a sound. I can't tell you what I felt. I was beyond any possibility of emotion.

"Come on," he whispered, jerking at my shoulder, desperation creeping into his voice. I don't know whether he felt he had to act with some urgency or whether I was letting down the side by showing weakness in front of the natives.

"They killed her," I managed at last. "They shot her down. It was an execution. They just took her out and shot her."

"I don't know anything about that," he said. "But we've got to get you out of here, fella." Tired as I was, that "fella" grated on my ears. It spoke of schools where the boys wore blazers with crests copied from Pall Mall packs, of hours spent practicing the piano, while Mom, cooking the food dad would eat when he returned from the office, monitored as she wiped the counter spotless. Had his wrestling coach called him "fella" before sending him onto the mat?

He might as well have called me "my good man." Where I came from, people didn't call one another "fella." It was the kind of thing Nelson Rockefeller shouted at voters when his motorcade stopped in the middle of a campaign tour. I looked up at him, knowing he was as much a foreigner to me as the uniformed men who surrounded him. Ashamed, I wanted to brush away my tears and my shoulders strained upward reflexively, but my hands were still cuffed behind my back.

"Let me get you someplace safe," and he resumed the tugging.

"There's an American woman inside that truck who was shot," I said, beginning to struggle to my feet. "She's right over there. All you have to do is push back the flap of the truck and you'll see her."

"I came here with the permission of the Guatemalan government in answer to a request by Professor MacElwain that I look into your whereabouts. I'm not free to conduct any kind of search. Even in the

United States, I wouldn't be allowed to do so without a warrant which specified what I was looking for."

"Even in the United States…At the request of Professor MacElwain…" How the phrases rolled from his lips! Even now, after years of listening to university administrators, it makes me cringe. Perhaps he knew she was there and had prepared himself for every eventuality. Perhaps it was just his schooling, his long hours at Georgetown University and his training in the foreign service.

"Look," I began, starting unsteadily for the truck. One of the officers grabbed me and began pushing me toward the door at the end of the garage.

"If you have charges to make, you may file them with the ambassador's secretary in the morning," said Furnival. "For now, you'd better concentrate on cooperating, or I'll never be able to get you out of here."

They hustled me to a room that was the duplicate of the one where Villa-Alba had interrogated me in Palin. The walls were the same institutional green, the same government desk, and the wooden chairs that had left similar scrape marks against the walls. MacElwain was sitting on the desk, smoking a Belmont. He looked remarkably at home.

"I'll just leave Mr. Fletcher here with you," Furnival said. He stepped from the room and the two of us were alone. One guard unlocked my handcuffs, and the two of them left as I tried to shake some feeling back into my hands. I wondered if Villa-Alba was in the next room, looking through a peephole.

"Jim," MacElwain said in the same stuffy tone he had used in the hotel. "I'm making arrangements to get you back to Berkeley. I'm afraid it will be impossible for you to continue doing your research here."

"They've shot Simone," I blurted. "The police executed her along with the Indian from Tecpan."

"From what they've told me," he said, "she had got herself mixed up with some local radicals. It's truly unfortunate. My job is to keep you from being implicated."

"Radicals? She was in a mission with a bunch of priests and nuns. God only knows what has happened to them."

"I've been assured that all of those who were actually in the mission building were safeguarded. If people who have been warned to stay inside insist on going out, then there's nothing that can be done for them. But you've got to stop talking about the people in the mission."

"You seem to know a great deal about what happened in Tecpan already," I said. "I'm sure your good friend Villa-Alba must have filled you in."

"Right now it's your safety I'm worried about," he said. "If, as you say, this young woman was murdered by the National Police, then you must know they wouldn't stop at executing you either. I think I can get you out of here, but you're going to have to do exactly as I say."

"What are you?" I asked. "Some kind of spy? Why should you let me out? I'm sure the faculty at Berkeley are going to be very excited when I tell them your research is just a front. When this comes out, you're going to be history. There will be so many protestors you won't be able to get to your office."

I have to give him credit. He never missed a beat, and the eyes enlarged by those obscene, round, wire-rimmed glasses didn't even flicker with emotion. "I'm going to leave you alone for a while," he said. "Of course, you are free to say whatever you like. But I suspect that once you think it over, you'll realize that whatever you say, you can't bring that young woman back to life or have the slightest impact on events."

He turned, walked through the door, closed it behind him, and I could hear the rasp of the lock. Five seconds later, the light in the room went out. Apparently, the switch was outside in the hall.

I fumbled my way to the door and tried the handle, but of course it was locked. The crack under the door illuminated nothing more than two inches of the concrete flooring. I stumbled back to the desk and transferred my allegiance to it.

With MacElwain gone, I had nothing to focus my anger. I was too tired to be afraid. In the end, I crawled up on the desk, curled on my right side using my arm for a pillow, and made an inventory of my body. My nose throbbed with dull persistence and I felt bruises on my left hip and arm. I must have scraped my forehead when I fell from the truck because my brow wouldn't wrinkle when I scrunched my eyes shut. Overwhelming all of these sensations, was the persistent ache of fatigue. Somewhere in the process of this accounting, I fell asleep.

Images stormed through my dreams in an incoherent jumble. The dead man in the truck. Simone's face expressionless. The fall forward onto the road. And with it all, the pain in my body as it stiffened on the bare surface of the metal desk.

The lights went on in the room and I found myself groggily trying to sit up. The diplomat had returned. I had no idea how long I had slept, but it couldn't have been long. To judge by the state of Mr. Furnival's summer suit, it might have been fifteen seconds. The man seemed to be protected by a force field which zapped any particle of dust that dared to soil him.

"What did you say to Doctor MacElwain?" he asked. "For a while I was afraid he was going to storm out of the building. I've never seen him so angry."

"Have you seen him often? I was told he hadn't been here for years."

"He contacted me the minute he got to Guatemala," he replied. "We've had a number of conversations since that time."

He was too quick in his response and I knew he was lying. "I bet you have," I said.

"Mister Fletcher, you're not making this easy. You may not realize it, but you are in great danger. The professor and I have no status in dealing with the police. In fact," and he leaned forward as if imparting classified information, "I could be subject to disciplinary action for entering this building."

"What could happen to you? Will the ambassador call you into his office foe a tongue lashing? A letter of reprimand in your file? Maybe you could have at one another with your old fraternity paddles. Could actually enhance your career, if he's that kind of a guy."

"Look," he said, "I'm not here because I like you, so being disagreeable isn't going to put me off. I'm here because it's my job to get American citizens out of trouble. You can't make me do anything else, no matter how you behave. If, as you charge, there is an American citizen who has been murdered, then the proper authorities will conduct an investigation and make a report. You will have an opportunity to be part of the process if you cooperate."

"There's not going to be any report," I said. "There aren't any authorities in the world. No one would listen to me. The best I could get would be an interview in the *New York Times* and an official denial from the State Department. Not even the Pope would touch this one. You're all in it together."

"We're not such bad people," he said. "The United States isn't such a bad country. It's not easy, when you have to deal with foreign countries. There are issues of nationalism and sovereignty. But if you don't wait too long, we may be able to arrange something. If you'll excuse me."

"You're a bunch of fuck heads, all of you," was the best I could manage.

He was unassailable, locked in the delicious novelty of his role. No matter how I behaved, all I could ever be was an anecdote traded among foreign service people at the bar. He would tell his buddies how stupid and obstinate I had been. They would shake their heads knowingly. There was no end to the foolishness of Americans overseas, they would agree. Now the Brits are different, used to this sort of thing, and the Germans, well, the Germans are impossible in any context. No, the Germans are OK as long as there is a supply of Mueslix around. The Swiss Embassy have it flown in in the diplomatic pouch. The conversation would drift away as contacts that could be vital to one's later career were being solidified.

The light stayed on, and however long I had slept, I wasn't going to sleep again. There was a crack in the plaster that looked like a profile of Hitler if you ignored that once it was past his chest it meandered diagonally to the floor. The desk had a metal rim which only ran around three quarters of the perimeter. One of the legs on the chair was shorter than the others but if you leaned back against the wall you could sit without rocking. This must be what it is like to be in prison.

For three hours -- at least I think it was three hours, for my watch had disappeared in the course of the evening -- the door remained resolutely shut. Twice the sound of footsteps in the hall brought me to my feet, but nothing came of it.

I had been a fool to antagonize MacElwain. If he really was a spy, he would be the only person with the leverage to get me out of here. These people would as soon shoot me as let me go. Now I had made myself the one person who could blow his cover. There was nothing to be done. Mostly I just wanted some fresh air.

Finally, I stood up. "OK," I announced to the unseen watchers who must have been monitoring me. "I'll do whatever you want."

Two minutes later, the knob rattled. I cringed into a corner, suddenly taken with the idea that soldiers were going to drag me out and shoot me. Had they been sent, just minutes before, on a mechanical errand of obliteration? I am ashamed to admit I was glad to see MacElwain's familiar bulk in the opening, with just the shoulder of Furnival's summer suit behind him. MacElwain gave me a calm, searching look as I stood, immobilized by fear.

"You'll begin by signing a written statement which I've drawn up," he said. "Then Furnival will debrief you."

Furnival cleared his throat. "If your behavior is adequate, we may have you meet with television reporters later in the day."

"No," said MacElwain, with a tone of curt command. "The priest will be the only one to meet with the press."

He turned from the doorway. "As I told you, it usually takes about three hours," he remarked to Furnival before he disappeared down the hallway.

EPILOGUE

I exceeded MacElwain's three hours by seventeen minutes. I have lived with those minutes ever since. In the earlier years, I was inclined to regard them as evidence of just how trivial and cowardly I was. I managed to dump Simone in a time statisticians would describe as less than significant deviation from the mean. In recent years, my mind has changed. I think now Simone would have found six hours and seventeen minutes more than adequate. She would have derided anyone who died for love in a foreign prison, sacrificing his life to the memory of another. She would have sneered at the idea of facing a firing squad and refusing the blindfold. Life goes on, and Simone was full of life. At least this is what I tell myself now, and if it makes me feel better to think so, where's the harm in that?

I discovered the seventeen minutes while sitting in a pleasant office in the American Embassy, the kind that have a seating area complete with sofa and coffee table on one side and a desk for the conduct of business on the other. The rug had the seal of the department of state (or was it of the whole United States?) in the center. Furnival was fiddling with the television monitor while I was preparing to sign my statement. MacElwain, ever the meticulous researcher, had attached a schedule of my interrogation at the National Police garage, saying I was transferred to an "accommodation room" at 5:45 AM central standard time and I had indicated my desire to make a statement at 12:02 PM. When I was in the room, I had imagined the world was dark around me. By the time my debriefing was complete, the late afternoon sun was slanting in the windows at the far end of the office.

The statement was a magnificent piece of fiction, a work of art that began with the admission that I exploited my research as an opportunity for small scale drug trafficking. This, MacElwain explained in a calm voice, would enable the government to prosecute me should I have any inclination to change my account of what happened. Simone, the statement said, knew nothing of my activities, or why I asked her to accompany me to meet with the communists who were heavily involved in the drug trade.

"This is bullshit," I said to MacElwain, "Nobody going to do a drug deal would take along a witness."

"You feared a double-cross," said MacElwain, "and you felt they wouldn't hurt a papal volunteer."

"But this makes me responsible for her death."

"It is extremely unlikely that this statement will ever be made public. Father Michael, um, what's his name, Corcoran will prove very convincing. He's outraged the Communists would kill an innocent woman out for an evening stroll. Your statement will simply provide back-up should any unanticipated anomalies develop concerning his testimony."

"And my statement will also serve to impeach my credibility in case I should happen to tell the truth about who actually killed Simone."

He looked at me with a calm expression. "As far as I am concerned, the evidence is clear that the Communist rebels killed the young woman. We have two sworn statements which corroborate the National Police's inquiry into the events."

"Here we go," said Furnival, sitting back from the television. Father Mike's awkward features appeared on a grainy background as he took questions from the assembled reporters.

"At about what time did the Communist attack begin on the village?" came a voice from off screen.

"Within a few minutes of the time our housekeeper, Maria, came to warn us of the attack. She returned to the mission at nine o'clock because she heard rumors that men were seen outside the village. It was her idea that we all hide in the cookhouse behind the patio. It saved our lives."

"And kept you safely out of range where you couldn't see who was doing the killing," I said aloud.

Furnival gave a jerk. "None of that," he said in an uncharacteristically firm tone.

"And the papal volunteer had left the mission prior to then?"

"Yes, she wanted to go for a walk alone. There was no way to reach her once the shooting began."

What had become of me? Apparently they had coached him that I was to play no part in the story.

"Wasn't she afraid to go out at night?"

"She was a wonderful young woman, well-liked in the village," at this point Father Mike's voice began to choke up, "because she loved and respected the people so much. She often went out alone."

"I see what you are doing," I said to Furnival. "Simone becomes a martyr in the cause, an innocent who wandered far from home in her desire to help others."

"The people in Washington think it's nice to have a model of a good young person to contrast to the hippy protestors who are burning down the campuses," said Furnival. "You know, Americans love youth, and in a time of inter-generational dispute, it is best not to have everyone on your side over fifty. This could help the war effort by showing how decent patriotic Americans act."

"Aren't you running a big risk? What if I say I was her lover? What if she wrote letters saying what a load of crap she thought the government was down here?"   "You won't tell anyone because no one will listen," he said. "No one in the United States cares about Guatemala. Ninety per cent don't even know where it is. At most you're talking about forty-five seconds on the evening news."

Furnival was wrong. Simone never made the evening news. A chemical plant in the Midwest burned, delaying traffic on a major interstate highway and providing spectacular pictures of motorists running for cover while smoke and flames roiled into the sky. I guess Father Mike wasn't photogenic enough while denouncing the communist attack on Tecpan. Who knows? Maybe if his family could have afforded orthodontia, my story would be different.

Furnival accompanied me on my flight back to the Bay Area, and he spoke with great bitterness on the power of the broadcasters to overlook his efforts. I think a public relations coup might have helped his career, though as far as I could see he was certainly efficient in his services to the state. I've lived long enough to know service is not a guarantee of advancement, and I wonder whether Furnival ever acquired the maturity to overcome life's unfairness. I hope he didn't, and he finished his career handling the shipment of oil executives' pets through quarantine in Abu Dhabi, but this is probably too much to ask of a random universe. Still, justice occasionally rains down along with injustice, and it certainly could have happened.

Upon my return to Berkeley, I made a few attempts to tell my story to the alternative press, but after brief indications of interests, journalists' efforts flagged. If Simone had been a committed revolutionary leader, they suggested, her death would be a tragedy worth writing about. I think part of the problem was her religion, making her unattractive to a left-wing audience. The rest of the problem was my inability to make her something more than she was. In the end, I gave up the effort. To see her enshrined as a second Rosa Luxembourg would be worse than letting her die unknown.

I was forced to see a great deal of MacElwain in the months after my return. To my amazement, he pretended my data was sufficient to support a PhD and treated me with a formal courtesy at the office meetings during which we edited my thesis, even accepting without demur the concluding paragraph that laid out the complete absence of support for thermal determinisim. Maybe he was afraid if he failed me and I appealed, his activities might come to light in a faculty which neither liked him personally nor felt any sympathy for his cause. Neither of us ever mentioned Simone until the final afternoon when I stopped by the office to have a copy of

the completed dissertation signed for the graduate
college office.

He was seated at his battered steel case desk, one
not unlike those in the offices of the Guatemalan
National Police. He looked up at me in the doorway but
made no invitation for me to enter. I advanced
uncertainly, holding the unbound dissertation in front of
me to make my intentions clear, almost as if I were
offering a steak to a ferocious dog.

"Well," I said, "It's done." After a pause I
added, "Here's the copy for you to sign."

"I understand New Mexico State made you an
offer for an assistant professorship," he said blinking
though the lenses of his glasses.

"The salary is standard," I said, "They have a
research station in the Sangre de Cristo Mountains so I'll
be able to escape the heat in the summer."

Another pause. It was the time for me to express
a student's appreciation for all his help, but I was
damned if I was going to say that. Similarly, he was
unwilling to indicate what a pleasure it had been to have
me as a student.

"It might be a good idea to work within the
United States," he said. "The world being what it is.
Americans get in trouble when they go overseas. They
forget they aren't at home and think they can go out
whenever they want. The young woman you knew…"

"Simone."

"Yes, that young woman. It's a shame she died.
They say she was very bright, if somewhat
unconventional."

I was frightened I would say something to betray her memory, but unwilling to say anything to annoy him, for he still could refuse to sign my thesis and my job was contingent upon its acceptance. He was expecting the conversation to go on, but I was dumb. Finally, he broke the silence.

"You probably should get this over to the graduate college," he said, scratching a ball point negligently across the signature page, and he handed the draft back to me.

"Yes," I said, and beat my retreat. As I went down the hall, I felt a thrill of freedom in the realization I never would have to speak to him again. It was the same freedom I felt on the first day I rode with Father Mike and Simone out of Guatemala City and into the highlands. No enchanted garden opened before me as I left the building, just the familiar gray shapes of Berkeley's architecture. It was a beginning, none the less.

I had one more stop to make before I could leave Guatemala behind.
In late August, after I'd driven my U-haul truck of personal possessions to New Mexico, I took a plane to Pittsburgh and hitchhiked east on Route 22 to Altoona. A trucker hauling a load of cigarettes dropped me off three blocks from the center of town at six in the morning and I walked down tree lined streets looking for a diner that. The only one I found didn't open until half past the hour, so I stood on the front steps in the warm light of an August morning.

Altoona was a railroad town in the nineteenth century and going to seed with the decline of industry, but the maples and tulip trees obscured the decay. Brick houses with white wood trim and drooping front porches sat behind shaded lawns. In the early morning sunshine, the town looked idyllic, if a little tawdry. A paper boy, pumping to move his load up even the modest grade made a right turn and began the long glide down a side street. It was easy to imagine Simone as a girl, pedaling her bike along the uneven pavement, the trees arching from both curbs to meet above her head as if she were traveling down a sun splashed tunnel.

When the diner opened, I bought coffee to take out, looked up the Duplesis address in the phone book, got directions from the waitress, and headed off on foot. I was enchanted by the stillness of the morning, cool enough at this hour though the day was going to be a scorcher. That morning Altoona seemed like a dream of small-town America, friendly and serene. Who would exchange this for the harsh ethnic wars of Guatemala, no matter how exotic and beautiful that land might be?

Adler Street, when I reached it, showed a little of the underside of Altoona society. The lawns were just as neat, almost rigidly trimmed in lower middle-class propriety, but the houses were small frame dwellings and the paint was peeling on many of the eaves. The peaked roofs marched in uniform rows down both sides of the street, suggesting the original tenants had been railway workers in company housing. Despite the occasional interruption of an addition covered with aluminum siding, the Pennsylvania Railroad stamp lay on all the inhabitants equally. Simone's house looked like all the rest, and I wondered whether Tommy lived up the street or down. Simone had never told me his last name, so there was no way to tell which house was his.

My pilgrimage was complete, and I wondered why I had come and what I expected to see. Still, the sight of her house was comforting. In the months since her death, she had begun to slip away from me. Sometimes it was hard to remember just how her face looked or what color her eyes were. Seeing this house and knowing she had actually run up and down those stairs made her real again, and I tried to engrave her on my memory.

Suddenly the door opened and a burly, dark haired man of about my own age emerged. He trotted purposefully down the steps, strode down the walk, and came out into the street toward me.

"Can I help you with something?" he asked. His tone was brusque. "You've been staring at my parents' house for the last ten minutes, and I wondered if you might want something." The words were pleasant enough, but the message was a clear "What the hell are you doing here?"

I tried not to appear evasive. "I happened to be passing through town and I thought I'd come by and look at the house. I knew your sister in Guatemala." At seven in the morning, this didn't sound very likely. "I'm terribly sorry about her death," I added lamely.

He had a hard time concealing his incredulity. "You were with the Mission?"

"No, no, I was just a researcher who stopped by a few times, but Simone and I got to know one another pretty well." Tantalizingly, the image of Simone accosting me outside the shower flashed back through my mind. Did everything I say have to sound like a fabrication?

"You'll have to come in and talk with my mother."

I was not prepared for this. I had come on my silent pilgrimage with the intention of seeing Altoona, maybe visiting her grave if I could find it, and then going away forever. The last thing I wanted was to talk about Simone. I had come to say farewell and now I was being pulled back.

"I really shouldn't," I said. "It's awfully early and I just came by because I happened to be passing through."

"Mom would kill me if I came back and said 'Oh, the guy watching our house was a friend of Simone's from Guatemala,'" he said. "It's been so hard on her, you know."

"I'm sure it must be, but I really can't."

Still, I let myself be led across the stoop and into the house. I noted Patrick, for Patrick it turned out to be, wiped his feet carefully on the mat as we entered, so I stopped to do so as well.

"It's a guy who knew Simone in Guatemala," Patrick announced in the tiny entry hall as soon as the door was open.

Simone's mother came out from the kitchen, wiping her fingers on a towel before she shook my hand. She wore an apron over her housedress, the kind with pockets big enough to hold a pair of scissors or some other necessary tool of housework. Her accent had a slight suggestion of a French-Canadian childhood. Her hair was pulled back in a twist and both the dress and the apron had been ironed and starched. At what hour she had risen to perform those secret rituals of bathing, combing, brushing, and dressing I could only guess, but I sensed they were as vital to her as eating or saying the rosary.

"You've met Patrick," she said. "My husband is working on a site near Uniontown and won't be home until the weekend. Patrick lives with his wife near Ebensburg. He just stayed over the night with me."

I guessed there was trouble in Ebensburg. Maybe Patrick had lingered too long with a barmaid or come in late and drunk once too often. Maybe an argument had exploded into a fight. Good old Patrick. One thing was sure, I would hear no more about it.

She led me to the parlor, phenomenally clean with not a magazine (*Readers Digest, America*) out of place. A crucifix in execrable taste looked down from a wall. After a brief negotiation, it was settled that I wouldn't stay for breakfast, but would accept a cup of coffee. It was delivered, complete with a coaster. Patrick made his way upstairs to shower before heading back to his job in Ebensburg and, I imagined, a reconciliation with his wife in the evening.

With the battlefield cleared, we settled to the main task of the morning. I became a scientist who, traveling to the mountains to collect moths, had the custom of stopping in the mission to visit the generous and hospitable Padre Ramon. In the course of these visits, I made the acquaintance of Simone and been struck by what a fine young woman she was, beloved of the Indians and well liked by everyone who came in contact with her.

"She mentioned you in one of her letters," Simone's mother interjected. "I hadn't realized you were quite so far along in your studies."

I translated this as "I didn't know you were so much older than she".

"I have the letter here, if you would like to see it."

The letters were kept in a cardboard box in the lower drawer of the television stand. The paper had lost all its stiffness from having been opened and reread, and the folds were starting to wear. She handled them as if they were relicts, carefully refolding each and replacing it in its envelope until she found the one she wanted. She handed over the second page only. All three pages appeared to be one paragraph, which ran in a disjointed rush.

"I've met a boy, an American who studies butterflies or something," she had scrawled across the blue paper in green ink. "I hate to break this to you, but he was raised as a Lutheran. Poor Mommy! Even in a country that is ninety per cent Catholic, Simone manages to pal around with a Protestant. At least he's not a tourist. What's wrong with tourists, Mommy, is they never leave home. They ride through Tecpan, eating box lunches from the hotel and breathing air conditioning and wondering when they are going to find a toilet as clean as the one at Howard Johnson's in New Brunswick. If we could find a way to bottle smog and pump it to them in little doses, we could have a fortune. Yesterday Maria made the worst dinner." The paragraph carried on and I disappeared from view.

I looked up into those unflinching gray eyes.

"Thank you for coming by, Mister Fletcher," she said. "It was terribly hard on us losing Simone. If only she hadn't gone to Guatemala… but of course none of us knew."

'She was a remarkable young woman," I said.

"One time she called me from a summer job and said, 'Mommy, run out back quick. There's the most beautiful sunset.'" Her hands were working in her lap as she struggled to maintain control. "Well, she's with God now," she concluded with a snap.

"I really have to be going," I said, and she didn't argue. She would spend the afternoon, I was sure, praying to get Simone out of purgatory. She was not one to abandon the harsher realities of her church's teaching.

As I walked down the front steps, I caught the flicker of a curtain in the house next door. Behind the window lurked another bereaved woman willing to banish her child in the service of propriety, nursing her grievances against her neighbor. It had been an illusion to think I could come to Altoona, walk through no man's land, and escape reconnaissance by either side.

I turned the corner without looking back and made my way to Route 22, walking along the roadside until well after I was past the limits of the town. My ticket was open return, and I had no desire for the inevitable opening questions that began after you slid onto the seat of a hitched ride. Maybe I could get someone in a pick-up to let me ride in the back.

As I walked down the graveled berm past fields where Holsteins grazed, the serene prosperity of the country all about overwhelmed me. America stretched enormous in all directions, filled with two hundred million people intent on nothing more than the score of the Dodgers game or the special on toilet paper at Krogers. Unthinking, ineluctable, and productive, they were a force stronger than fate. The bland certainty of each day wound into the next until it crushed us or forced us into headlong flight.

Simone and I were exiles in an antique and impoverished land. We thought we had found freedom in Guatemala. We thought the conquistadores had crushed a civilization so low we could walk with impunity, armed only with the power of our industrialized currency and our North American arrogance. Simone created a little universe there where the sex was pleasurable and the future unanticipated.

On the shore of the ocean immemorial, we built our barricades of sand against the advancing tide. Bedazzled by the glitter of sunlight on the ripples, we thought nothing of the wrecks that line the bottom with coral crusted cannon and sea bleached bones. Ours was a world born each morning anew when the sunlight unfolds from the waves like a roseate fan. Until we learned, as all must in time, that the sea will never give up its dead; the past cannot release its thralls.

www.ingramcontent.com/pod-product-compliance
Lightning Source LLC
Chambersburg PA
CBHW061525120726
48001CB00004B/1403